CAROLINE

Cornelius Medvei was born in 1977 and grew up in the east of England. He studied modern languages at Oxford University and worked for a time in China as a teacher. His first book, *Mr Thundermug*, was published in 2006. He lives in London.

CORNELIUS MEDVEI

Caroline

A Mystery

VINTAGE BOOKS
London

Published by Vintage 2012

2 4 6 8 10 9 7 5 3

First published in Great Britain in 2011 by
Harvill Secker

Vintage
Random House, 20 Vauxhall Bridge Road,
London SW1V 2SA

www.vintage-books.co.uk

Addresses for companies within The Random House Group Limited
can be found at: www.randomhouse.co.uk/offices.htm

The Random House Group Limited Reg. No. 954009

A CIP catalogue record for this book
is available from the British Library

ISBN 9780099548683

The Random House Group Limited supports The Forest Stewardship
Council® (FSC®), the leading international forest-certification organisation.
Our books carrying the FSC label are printed on FSC®-certified paper.
FSC is the only forest-certification scheme supported by the leading
environmental organisations, including Greenpeace. Our
paper procurement policy can be found at
www.randomhouse.co.uk/environment

MIX
Paper from
responsible sources
FSC® C016897

Printed and bound in Great Britain by Clays Ltd, St Ives PLC

To my parents

1

I was contemplating the view from my office window one winter afternoon when the receptionist came in with a parcel for me. It was a bulging manila envelope, torn at the seams and encrusted with packing tape.

I set about opening the parcel with a paper knife. Inside, I found a disorderly bundle of documents. At the top of the pile was an academic paper on the relative merits of maize and beet as fodder crops, with some impenetrable statistics relating to soil types and yields. While maize had a greater calorific value pound for pound, beet was more easily digestible. Maize offered a higher potential yield per hectare, but beet was more tolerant of poor soils . . . The paper broke off before it reached a conclusion, and there followed a lengthy excerpt from a private journal describing some sort of emotional crisis, the precise nature of which was not made clear. 'Something of a young Audrey Hepburn about her,' I remember one note ran, 'gamine

– wide-eyed.' This journal ended as abruptly as the academic paper had done, and with some relief I found myself reading a detailed account of the chess match between Roessler and Ladanyi in Carlsbad in 1923 (notable, apparently, for Ladanyi's victory by means of a double bishop sacrifice, as well as for his successful use of a line in the French Defence that had previously been considered unsound).

There was more; several hundred pages, in fact, and all of it interleaved with old utility bills, shopping lists and sweet wrappers. The papers appeared to have been hurriedly swept together and crammed into the envelope. I looked in vain for a covering letter; there wasn't even a sender's address, although my own name and address were clearly printed in black felt tip. I shook the envelope, and some yellowed chess problems clipped from a newspaper fluttered out.

Even after reading this far, I was no closer to understanding what it was all about, and part of my brain told me that I might as well look for meaning and coherence in the contents of the waste-paper basket. But I went on studying the papers until it was time to go home.

The parcel had been a welcome distraction, of course, but there was more to it than that. As I sit here in the offices of the *Evening News*, studying company reports and economic forecasts, the entire fabric of the city outside is being torn apart and reassembled in a strange new guise – it makes me think of a man trying to put on a new jacket while still struggling out of the one he was wearing. Even from my window I have a view of a construction site: the office block across the road was recently pulled down, and now you look out onto a field of rubble. On the far side there is a row of low-rise shops and canteens and behind them, in the distance, a view of the tall buildings in the new district across the river. Seen through the peculiar mixture of river mist and industrial pollution that covers the city in winter for weeks at a time, they appear as dim, insubstantial forms, like the ink-and-wash mountains in an old watercolour.

I have all the facts – I know, for example, that the city's population has increased from 3 to 8 million in the space of twenty years, that the metropolitan area has grown from 105 square kilometres in 1990 to 340 square kilometres today, and that last year alone, according to a report by the Urban Planning Department, more than 700,000 cubic metres of concrete were poured, 2 million square metres of low-rise housing stock were demolished and 260,000 households relocated to the outer suburbs. But the more information I assemble, the more confused everything becomes, until I begin to despair of ever making sense of this city, which is expanding furiously and at the same time collapsing under its own weight, which seems less fit for human habitation the more crowded it becomes, and where I feel more of a stranger with every day that passes.

But the arrival of this parcel had put an odd idea into my head. As I pored over the chaotic bundle of papers, it occurred to me that they might contain an answer to my problems. There was no sensible reason to believe that an incongruous mixture of references to agricultural engineering and chess tactics and an Audrey Hepburn lookalike would succeed in shedding light where solid journalism and reams of carefully compiled statistics had failed. Nevertheless, the two problems were connected in my mind: here at last, I felt, was a mystery equal to the mystery of the city itself. I was sure that, at the very least, investigating the contents of the parcel would distract me for a while from fretting about the city, but I also had the wild hope that if I could get to the bottom of the mystery on my desk I would gain an insight into the one outside my window.

The following afternoon I was trying to concoct a light and engaging article out of a press release about a convention of footwear manufacturers when the phone rang and the receptionist said that Mr Shaw wanted to speak to me.

I knew several Mr Shaws: Mr Shaw the advertising editor, Mr Shaw from the City Council, Mr Shaw my downstairs neighbour.

'It's me – you remember?'

His voice was certainly familiar, but it took me a moment
to place him. It was none of the Mr Shaws I had in mind,
but an old classmate from middle school. We'd been quite
good friends then, but since leaving school we'd lost touch
altogether. I asked him what he was doing these days, and he
explained that he was working for a small import-export firm
– he'd been out of the country for several years.

'Did you get the parcel I sent?'

'So it was *you* who sent those papers?'

'Of course.' He sounded surprised. 'Didn't you read my letter?'

'There wasn't a letter.'

'There wasn't? I know I wrote one – I must have forgotten to
put it in . . .' He began to apologise for his absent-mindedness,
while I stared out of the window. It had started to rain, and the
construction workers, in wellington boots, splashed through
the pools of water that were collecting in the trenches and hol-
lows.

'Anyway,' he said at last, 'I wondered if you were busy this
week?'

We met the following day, at the subway exit on the corner
near my office. It was still raining, a fine needling drizzle: I
shook out my umbrella and scrutinised the crowd sheltering
inside the doorway. I wondered if Shaw would have changed
much, but when he arrived a few minutes later, running up the
steps, I recognised him at once.

He was still as skinny as I remembered him, a little fuller
in the face perhaps, and with the same nervous, bobbing

gait, bouncing off the balls of his feet. He thanked me for meeting him, seized my hand and shook it energetically, but he seemed preoccupied and wasted no time on small talk. He set off quickly down the street, and as I followed, struggling to keep up with him, I remembered how he always used to be in a hurry, as if he had urgent business somewhere. We went into the first restaurant we came to, not much more than a canteen, with the kitchen just inside the entrance.

'You're wondering about the papers,' he said, after the waiter had brought us a bottle of beer and two glasses, and taken our order. 'Well, they're my father's memoirs. At least, that's what he called them.'

'I see,' I said carefully, noting the past tense.

'He died – I came home for the funeral last week.'

'I'm sorry.' I asked him how it had been, and he leant animatedly across the rickety table, making the sauce bottles rattle in their cruet. The ceremony, he said, had been disappointing. He had arrived late; as he took his seat, he had surveyed the assembled mourners and recognised nobody. He described the order of service – which according to his mother had been chosen by the priest, and according to the priest had been chosen by his mother – with musical accompaniment provided by an uncle; and the readings, which were by turns excessively moralising and excessively flippant, but above all completely unrepresentative of his father's tastes.

'Well,' the priest had said, when Shaw accosted him afterwards, 'what would have been representative of your father's tastes? It certainly wasn't my idea to have someone playing the saxophone.'

But the worst part of the ceremony, he told me, had been the tributes from various neighbours and colleagues of his father.

'Why, what did they say?'

'Oh, that he was hard-working, and a family man, and fond of a joke, that sort of thing . . .'

'It wasn't true?'

'No, no, it was all true, but it had nothing to do with *him* – I mean, any of them could have taken his place in the coffin, we could have said the same words over their heads, and no one would have noticed any difference. There was something *missing*, if you see what I mean.'

I didn't. All these things were upsetting, certainly, but not enough to account for his distraught manner, the wild energy in his eyes. He leant across the table again; the sauce bottles began to rattle uncontrollably. 'And at last I saw what it was. At no point in the whole proceedings had anyone mentioned Caroline.'

He sat back with an air of triumph – like a teacher who has just proved a point, waiting for the pupil to catch up. But I had no idea who Caroline was. I expected that he would explain, but in his agitation he was growing incoherent.

'Afterwards there was a party at my parents' flat, and everyone had stories about him, as if they wanted to prove their credentials as his friends – stories I'd heard countless times before, and still nothing about Caroline.

'I couldn't understand why no one had mentioned her. At first I thought they must be embarrassed. Then I wondered if they were trying to be tactful – obviously they didn't want to upset my mother. But by the end of the evening I was beginning to think they'd simply forgotten all about her.'

Was he talking about another woman, I wondered, or an estranged daughter? But I didn't interrupt; he seemed to be working round to telling me a story. Over the years I have sat through enough recitals of deranged fantasy or open slander in the course of my work to make me wary in situations like this. All the same, I was very curious to hear what could possibly explain the collection of bizarre and ill-matched papers that he had sent me.

'The most tedious accounts of card games,' he went on, 'and office parties, and cautious youthful indiscretions, but nothing about the most remarkable episode in his life – the only remarkable episode in his life. Maybe you're wondering why I didn't say anything? Well, I didn't trust myself to open my mouth. I didn't know what would come out – whether I'd start telling them all exactly what I thought of them, or just burst into tears. And also, I must admit, by then I was wondering whether I'd remembered it all correctly. In the end I just slipped out to look in the hall cupboard, to prove to myself that she had really existed – to see her old blanket, and her nosebag.'

'Her nosebag?' I'd listened patiently – at first thinking that everything would become clear in due course, and then finding it impossible to get a word in – but I was still none the wiser as to who Caroline was, and this new information only confused things further.

'Did you actually read those papers?' he asked, seeing the expression on my face.

'I did,' I told him, 'but I must say I couldn't make much sense of them.'

'Well then,' he said, 'I should explain.'

What follows is Shaw's story, presented from his point of view, as I heard it from him that afternoon in the restaurant. I put it together furtively, in spare moments at the office. I was under no illusion that the editor would see it as suitable material for the paper – on the contrary, he would probably take it as an unnecessarily elaborate letter of resignation.

I have interspersed what Shaw told me with extracts taken from his father's papers – I wouldn't inflict the whole of that rambling, unintentionally self-revealing work of cribbed and half-baked scholarship on the reader. But I felt the need to corroborate the account, or at least to demonstrate that if it reads in places like the product of a deranged mind, it is not my mind that is deranged. In places, too, I have added a few editorial notes for the sake of clarity.

In my time as a journalist I have written many kinds of article: news reports, exposés, testimonies, human interest pieces. But this story did not really fit into any of those categories. It was hardly a news report, and to call it an exposé would be to imply that the matter had been deliberately covered up. 'Testimony' would have been presumptuous, since Shaw had not formally asked me to record the story, while the term 'human interest' was, in the circumstances, almost wilfully inaccurate.

In the end, I decided to call it *Caroline: A Mystery*, partly because her character was a mystery, as was her ultimate fate; but also because 'mystery' seems the best word to describe the whole extraordinary, inspiring affair – I mean in the sense that it seemed to contain a profound and important truth that could be glimpsed but perhaps never fully grasped or understood. But I am getting ahead of myself.

2

The summer before my father retired, my parents rented a house in the mountains north of the city. We always took our holidays at the same time, like everyone else, in the first weeks of August, when the city steamed like a midden and the summer heat had become almost unbearable. Shops and restaurants closed, offices emptied and the vast concourse of the main railway station was crammed with hunted-looking families surrounded by piles of bulky luggage. The streets in the city centre were almost deserted, while all the exit roads were choked with traffic. There was an atmosphere of licence and barely suppressed panic, as if the city was about to be overtaken by some great calamity.

Certainly this mood would infect my father, who always insisted on supervising our packing, but would end up leaving work unexpectedly late and having to do everything at the last minute. This set a mood of tension and urgency, which intensified as he strode from room to room flinging items into suitcases at random, as if the house was on fire and he was trying to save what he could. At last he would drag the luggage outside and spend an anxious half-hour trying to fit it all into the boot of our hired car, while my mother and I sat at the kitchen table eating sandwiches.

It was the same every year. As I grew older, I wondered why he had never managed to evolve a more methodical, relaxed approach to the whole enterprise, and why my mother put up with it so patiently. She would always withdraw behind a pile of ironing or run herself a bath while the packing was going on, having already put the things she needed in a small bag several hours beforehand. It seemed to me that if she had been in charge everything would have been done with less fuss and in half the time. But now I think she understood that it would have been useless to ask him to leave work on time, or to start getting ready a day or two earlier. A holiday is often described as an escape, or a getaway; for my father there was nothing metaphorical about these terms. On our family holidays he was in flight from his everyday life, and the panicked, hasty departure and the journey by night were for him an essential part of the proceedings.

When the last of the luggage had been jammed into the boot and my mother had locked up the house and watered the geraniums in the yard, we would get in the car and my father would drive carefully down the lane and out onto the main road holding the steering wheel with one hand and a sandwich with the other.

Now that we had made our escape, the mood lightened. My mother would produce a bag of mints and pass them round, and as we made our way through the streets we would see who could be first to spot a certain make of car, or a man with a beard, or an advertisement for hand cream. Once we were out of the city, my father would put some opera in the tape deck and make us laugh by miming along with the soprano's arias. When it got dark the mints would be passed round again and soon afterwards, lulled by the motion of the car, I would drift off to sleep.

Even if nothing else about that holiday had been particularly memorable, I would still have remembered the house we stayed in, which had until recently been the local school. It stood just outside the village, overlooking a lake, down a lane that ran through the woods a little way above the shore, with the water glinting below. Beyond it the lane ran on beside the lake for a while, then turned uphill between the trees.

The smaller of the two classrooms and the teachers' office had been turned into bedrooms. There was a lean-to kitchen, and the larger classroom, with its great window in the gable end, served as a living room. On the bookshelves, along with the usual assortment of battered paperbacks, I found the school atlas, a twenty-year-old encyclopedia missing several volumes, and an abridged translation of Buffon's *Natural History*. Outside, instead of a garden, was the cracked and mossy asphalt of the playground on which the faded markings of a basketball court were still just visible, while the playing field behind the house had reverted to a meadow – the goalposts sunk knee-deep in the grass.

Most of my friends spent their holidays on coach tours to celebrated beauty spots, or visiting relatives in other cities, so I think my parents' preference for cottages in remote parts of the countryside was considered slightly eccentric, but it was an arrangement that suited both of them. For my mother, who ran a small catering business from home, a holiday meant first of all a complete break from all culinary activity. She would sit outside in a folding chair in the shade, labouring over a crossword and getting up from time to time to change her position as the shadows crept across the grass. At her feet there was always a plastic shopping bag in which she kept such essential items as yesterday's newspaper, a roll saved from lunch, a cardigan, some unwritten postcards and an umbrella. This, together with the fact that she usually wore her oldest and most comfortable clothes, gave her the air of a derelict on a park bench, something that my father never tired of pointing out. My mother generally responded to his witticisms with dignified silence, but if there was a suitable missile in her bag – a bread roll, perhaps – she would throw it at him when he turned his back.

After a few days relaxing in this way, she liked to spend the rest of the holiday experimenting with new recipes, free from interruption by neighbours and clients. Admittedly, the limited resources of the various kitchens tested her ingenuity; some vital piece of equipment was usually missing, and she would find herself rolling out pastry with a beer bottle or using a biscuit tin as a jelly mould. Often, too, we had strange meals; in the first part of the holiday because my father was doing the cooking, and in the second, because my mother's schedule of experimentation took no account of conventional menu planning – there would be two kinds of soufflé for breakfast, or an evening meal composed entirely of canapés.

For my father, meanwhile, the summer holiday was an escape – a chance to discard, for a little while, his professional life. It was perhaps a natural consequence of this that he often found himself at a loose end, at least for the first day or two – the important thing for him was what he left behind, not what he did when he got to where we were going. But sooner or later he would come across one of the unexpected props that always seemed to turn up in those holiday cottages – a guitar behind the sofa, a fencing foil in the umbrella stand – which he seized on like a drowning man clutching a branch, and which kept him happily occupied for the rest of our stay. One year, when no ready-made distractions presented themselves, he devoted himself to growing a beard. He was so entirely convincing in this new context – fiddling with the guitar, surprising us by picking out 'House of the Rising Sun' or 'Scarborough Fair', or frying drop scones for breakfast on the gas ring – that his other life, in which he wore a suit and tie and left the house each morning at five to eight, was quickly consigned to the realm of hazy and faintly distasteful memory.

On that particular holiday, the short nights helped to give the impression that the normal pattern of life had been interrupted: this far north, in summer, one day runs into another almost without a break. For an hour or so around midnight, the shadows would lengthen, but that was all; everywhere the mild unfailing light on the village streets and gardens, on forests and upland meadows. We were exhilarated and slightly giddy, from lack of sleep and the sense of tremendous potential – as if all these extra hours, the daylight flooding the empty hillsides, might be harnessed somehow, put to use, like the water dammed up in the high valleys.

As for me, I spent the first day exploring the surrounding area, partly to see how the land lay, but also to find out if there were any other children in the neighbourhood. But I wandered round the village without meeting anyone my own age and then went down to the lake, where there were some promising-looking tents which I hoped might be occupied by families, but which turned out to belong to solitary men fishing for trout. It was then that I realised I would have to fall back on my own resources.

Back at the house I discovered that by clambering along the perimeter railings I could make a complete circuit of the playground and the meadow without touching the ground, and in this way I amused myself for a few hours. The next morning it was raining, and unable to go outside I spent hours climbing on the ropes and other gymnastic equipment that were still bolted to the walls of the living room. When I tired of this I stretched out on the vaulting horse that stood under the window and read the comics I had brought with me, while the rain pattered on the glass.

In the afternoon the rain stopped, and my mother suggested a walk up the lane behind the house. As the road turned uphill, it quickly left the woods and ran on between high hedges that enclosed a few tilting, sodden fields. Beyond them the ground rose more steeply, dotted with rocks and pine trees, before heaving itself up into a series of low but jagged peaks, which that afternoon were still smothered in cloud. I had run on ahead, and so I was the first to see her; round a bend in the lane the hedge was interrupted by a length of unsteady fencing, with a small field behind it. I hung on the gate to catch my breath, wondering what kind of animal might occupy this unpromising patch of cropped grass and thistles. Then I saw at the far end an old railway carriage half-buried in a clump of birch trees and, standing in the open doorway, a donkey, tossing its head and staring back at me.

My first reaction was one of pity; what kind of life could an animal have, I wondered, all by itself in this forlorn and isolated place?

At the same time I felt slightly disappointed; the summer evening had been so pregnant with possibility, the disruption of the laws of nature, as I understood them, so complete. I had the overactive imagination that sometimes goes with being an only child, and I suppose I was hoping for some kind of marvellous discovery – a cave full of treasure perhaps, or a couple of fairies. But all I had found was this donkey, which was remarkable only for the crushing contempt it managed to convey with a single twitch of its ears.

As I was considering all this my parents caught up with me, and leant over the gate to see what I was looking at.

'It's a donkey,' my father said.

As if to confirm this statement of the obvious, the donkey stepped out of the carriage doorway and trotted up to us, and it was then we saw that she was a female. She tossed her head and snorted, and stopped in front of my father.

They faced each other across the sagging gate. He saw a rusty grey, barrel-chested donkey, with pretty ears nine inches long (one cocked, the other drooping to the left), head on one side, flicking her tail to keep the flies away. I noticed her shaggy coat and the pale whiskers on her upper lip, and wondered how old she might be. I wasn't sure how you told a donkey's age; something to do with their teeth, I thought, but she kept her mouth firmly shut as she champed on a mouthful of grass in a manner that suggested intense concentration mingled with dumb insolence, like a bored teenager with a plug of bubblegum.

And she, fixing my father with her great, dark, limpid eyes – 'eyes a man could drown in', as he later described them – took in the hair thinning at the temples, his nose reddened with sunburn, his stomach bulging slightly over the waistband of his shorts (like all his colleagues, my father always wore shorts on holiday, regardless of the weather; shorts were not allowed in the office).

I suppose this was the moment when the whole strange affair began; the moment, so well documented in classical poetry and TV soaps and sugary ballads, when two strangers come face to face; the heart thumps, an overpowering force shakes them, like the wind in the birch trees above the stable – in short, they begin to fall for each other . . . An odd way, perhaps, to describe the first meeting, in a muddy field, of a middle-aged insurance broker and a donkey. But this was how it happened.

He put out his hand and stroked her ears; she submitted to this for a few seconds, then threw back her head and brayed. Perhaps in her girlish dreams a man exactly like my father had appeared, a stranger leaning on the gate; someone kind, attentive, but also firm and masterful, who would unfold for her the mysteries of the world that lay beyond this acre or so of poor grazing – or she may simply have enjoyed the feel of his soft office-worker's hands on her muzzle, so different from the rough caresses of a countryman. My mother patted her neck tentatively, but the donkey did not respond, and she ignored my efforts to tempt her with a handful of grass. All her attention was fixed on my father, who was gazing back at her with an expression of rapt concentration.

'She likes you,' said my mother.

With an effort my father roused himself from his reverie.

'I wonder what her name is,' I said.

'It's Caroline,' he said. 'Look, it's painted on the side of her house.'

'That might be the name of the train, or where the train was going,' my mother said.

'Don't be silly,' said my father. 'Who ever heard of a place called Caroline? No, it's her name all right.' And he stroked Caroline's ears again, while the donkey butted him coyly in the chest. 'There,' he said, 'you see? Caroline. That's right, isn't it?' He rubbed the back of his hand on her muzzle a little self-consciously, then leant on the gatepost and rested his chin on his arms, as if he was settling down for the rest of the afternoon.

'Well,' my mother said, 'shall we carry on? The shops close at five, if you were thinking of buying something for dinner.'

My father slowly stood up straight and stretched, but he showed no inclination to move, and he did not take his eyes off the donkey.

'You can always come back tomorrow,' my mother said. 'I'm sure Caroline will still be here.'

When we got back to the house, my father went straight to the bookshelves. He went outside with his arms full – luckily the volume *Dentine to Electroplating* was not missing from the encyclopedia – and for the rest of the afternoon he reclined in a deckchair in the playground, with a pile of books on the asphalt beside him, chewing on a straw and turning the pages with great concentration.

For dinner that evening my father made cheese omelettes, his signature dish. It was a indication of his distracted state that he managed to burn two of them on the bottom, while the fried potatoes he made to go with them were only half- cooked. Usually while were were eating he would ask us what we wanted to do the following day, or invite our comments on the food. But as we ate our omelettes that night he talked incessantly, comprehensively, and exclusively about donkeys. Perhaps we did not realise, he told us, in a tone of faint reproach, what a remarkable beast the donkey was.

Its digestive juices, for example: of course it was well known that the donkey converted fodder into energy more efficiently than any other quadruped, but were we aware that its stomach contained a mixture of nitric and hydrochloric acid in exactly the same proportions as the *aqua regia* used by medieval alchemists for dissolving gold? That in a laboratory experiment, liquid samples from a donkey's digestive tract had been found to dissolve hair, teeth, iron filings, and a gold wedding ring lent by a lab technician in the mistaken belief that it would just be thoroughly cleaned?

Its constitution: despite the donkey's hardiness in matters of diet, its ability to survive for weeks at a time on weeds and ditchwater, it was surprisingly sensitive to the wet. The donkey's coat was rough and absorbent; if it got wet through, it took a long time to dry. A donkey with a sodden coat was sure to catch a chill, and a chill in turn was sure to lead to pneumonia – the most common cause of death among domesticated stock. It might interest us to know, he said, that even the wild burros in the deserts of New Mexico took care not to stray too far from favourite caves or overhanging rocks where they could shelter from a downpour.

The length of its memory: whatever we might have heard about elephants and dolphins in this regard was largely fanciful, but there was extensive documentary evidence for the donkey's powers of recollection. There were accounts of elderly donkeys led for the first time in years past the farm where they had been born, pulling at the halter and trying to go in at the gate; a donkey attacking a stranger apparently without provocation and tearing strips off his jacket after recognising him as a former owner who, it transpired, had mistreated her fifteen years earlier; a circus donkey that memorised pi to forty-three decimal places.

While we cleared the table he rambled on, his eyes shining with the zeal of the new convert, lecturing us about *Don Quixote*. Sancho Panza standing by while his master tilted at windmills he attributed not to the servant's good sense but solely to the fact that, unlike his master, he had been mounted on a donkey. A horse might be persuaded to take part in such a pointless exercise, but a donkey never. The horse was vainglorious, flighty, easily led; but there always had to be a quid pro quo with a donkey. And no doubt we remembered the story of the emperor Caligula, whose appointment of a horse as consul was cited as conclusive proof of his insanity? If he had only had the good sense to offer the post to a donkey he might have gone down in history as a wise and enlightened ruler.

As my mother and I washed up, he wandered round the kitchen distractedly polishing a glass and lecturing us on the donkey's role in art through the ages. Its earliest appearance, he informed us, had been in the rock drawings of the Nubian desert, where the African wild ass had been the chief quarry of the prehistoric hunter-gatherers. On the reliefs and friezes in the tombs of Egyptian kings it was depicted principally as a beast of burden, driven by brutal overseers wielding sticks, bloody welts on its hindquarters, carrying sheaves of corn from the fields or trampling the grain on the threshing floor. It had an important place in the religious iconography of the Italian Renaissance, the presence of a donkey in a painting enabling its pallid and otherwise nondescript human companion to be identified as St Anthony of Padua, patron of the lost and shipwrecked.

There was something impressive, certainly, about the way he had managed to assimilate all his reading, although some of the claims he made struck me even then as being of doubtful veracity. He announced that the American

West had been won by the donkey, and the Industrial Revolution built on its back; the donkey had built the railroads and dug the mines, and George Washington had bred donkeys in his spare time. He talked of the donkey-headed gods of the Upper Nile and the sacred ass made of birch twigs which the ancient Prussians worshipped in their midsummer ceremonies. He lamented the donkey's use in war – the donkey-hide boots worn against snakebite by troops on jungle campaigns and, in earlier times, Samson smiting his enemies with the jawbone of an ass. It was regrettable, he said, that scripture did not reveal which part of the jawbone he had smitten them with – it was details such as this that were so valuable to the natural historian.

He did not seem in the least discouraged by our undisguised lack of interest. In this he resembled the many bores I would meet at dinner tables in later life, who mistake the marshalling of curious facts and scraps of trivia for interesting conversation. But unlike them, my father was not out to impress or entertain us. It was more as though he wanted to get something off his chest – although what exactly, I could not have said.

On the following day he mumbled an excuse about checking some of the facts that had come up in his reading and went up to the field again, taking with him a bag of radish tops and apple cores that he had saved from lunch. He did not return until the evening, chattering excitedly about how Caroline had preferred the apple cores to the radish tops – next time he would try her with cabbage leaves. There was no mention of the facts he had been so eager to verify; instead he pushed the kitchen table and chairs to one side and lay down on the floor, kicking his legs in the air and rubbing his shoulders vigorously against the linoleum, in order to demonstrate exactly how Caroline had rolled in the dusty patch by the gate. It was not until much later that I recognised his outlandish monologue for what it had really been: a declaration of love.

The donkey, Equus asinus, is neither a creature of fable nor of history like the unicorn or the dodo, so it may seem unnecessary to offer a detailed description, especially when it has been done so many times before. I am more concerned – as all good scholars must be – with the shortcomings of previous scientific and literary accounts. Buffon's Natural History offers perhaps the classic anatomical description:

'The lower part of the ass's head, reading from the eyes to the extremity of the lips, is not equal in length to that of the horse, in proportion to the space between the eyes and the ears. Nor is this excess only in length, it is also wider and flatter. Besides, the ears being longer, more vacillating, and hanging lower, give the ass a heavy, stupid look; while, by the difference we observed in these parts of the horse, the latter acquires an air of elegance and sagacity. The heavy head, the long flapping ears, the large and thick neck, the contracted chest, the arched and sharp back, the haunches being raised above the withers, the flattened croup, the bare tail, and crooked hind-legs, altogether render the appearance of the ass mean and contemptible.'

The individual details cannot be faulted. But note the bizarre and frankly insulting conclusion. 'Mean and contemptible' indeed! It is as if he had added up all the parts of a sum but produced the wrong answer. This is compounded by the specious and entirely unscientific comparison with Equus caballus. To continue:

'Instead of the air of good humour and docility so pleasing in the horse, the large head on the ass, the long and thick hairs which cover its forehead and temples, its hollow eyes, and their distance from each other, with the muzzle swelling towards its extremity, give the ass a look of heaviness and stupidity.'

It is regrettable to see subjective aesthetic judgements of this kind presented as scientific facts, especially by a natural historian. We do not assume that beauty in humans is a sign of intelligence – if anything, rather the reverse. Why, then, should the donkey's unconventional good looks be taken as evidence of stupidity? If, sir, you had taken the trouble, as I did, actually to look – to gaze – into those 'hollow eyes', instead of measuring the distance between them, you could never have made such an assertion...

But Buffon's comments on the donkey's character are nearer the mark:

'By his natural temper he is as humble, as patient, and quiet as the horse is proud, fiery and impetuous; he bears with firmness, and perhaps with courage, blows and chastisements...(1) Why then should this creature, so mild, so patient, so sober, and so useful, be so much despised?'

Why indeed? The donkey submits itself, without complaint, to a life of drudgery. It takes on the unglamorous hack work and the unpaid overtime and is rewarded, if it is noticed at all, with perfunctory and faintly contemptuous thanks and a list of further duties. But if it stops working, even for a moment, or takes a day off sick, then the poor beast receives a vicious cut across the rump, or a threat of disciplinary proceedings from its line manager.

'Do men, even in animals, condemn those who serve them too well and too cheaply?(2) The horse is trained up, great care is taken of him, he is instructed and exercised, while the poor ass is left to the brutality of the meanest servant, and the wantonness of children... He is the sport, the butt, the drudge of clowns; who, without the least thought or concern, drive him along with a cudgel, striking, overloading and tiring him.'

(1) See for example Savory, E.W. (1921) <u>Across the Himalaya by Donkey-Cart</u>. Simla: Powell and Martin. pp. 43, 108, 152, 163, 171, 176, 179, 180, 181.
(2) See Grunhardt, P. (1983) 'The Provenance of Meat Derivatives in Commercial Dog Food.' <u>Journal of Canine Nutrition</u> 34:3.

3

As the days passed and my father's attachment to Caroline showed no sign of weakening, my mother and I became anxious. The return to everyday life could be a difficult time for him. Of course, it is not unusual to regret the end of a pleasant holiday, but for my father the idea of being reunited with his suit and his desk was enough to induce a mood of deep gloom – worse still was the thought that in a few days he would be so thoroughly absorbed again by his routine as to have all but forgotten this brief period of liberation, and with nothing to show for it but a peeling nose and a few photographs. I thought again of the year when he had grown a beard; he had been too upset to shave it off himself on the last evening, and my mother had to do it for him. I still remember him sitting forlornly at the kitchen sink – my mother was keeping half an eye on a batch of meringues – while the tears trickled down through the shaving soap on his cheeks.

In the last few days he spent more and more time up in the donkey's field, and when he was with us he was uncharacteristically withdrawn and restless. On the last night he was late for supper, and my mother was on the point of sending me out to look for him when he came in grinning, unable to keep still, brimming with barely contained euphoria. The story came out in a rush.

When he went to see Caroline that evening, another man had been there already, leaning on the gate and gazing into the field. Beyond a brief nod, the stranger did not respond to my father's greeting, but watched as the donkey approached the gate and forced her head between the bars to get at the quartered apple my father was holding out to her.

'A fine animal,' he remarked gravely, as Caroline munched on the pieces of apple one after the other.

'She certainly is,' my father said.

'She likes a nice apple,' said the stranger, reaching out and scratching the donkey's neck. 'Good for the coat, apples are.'

(Incidentally, my father told us afterwards, this was complete nonsense.)

'Try her with a spring onion, though,' the man went on. 'She'll do anything for a spring onion.'

'Is that so?' my father said, a little irritably – this man and his inconsequential remarks were intruding on his precious last moments with Caroline. 'Well, as it happens I didn't bring any spring onions with me.' And he began to fish distractedly in his pocket for another apple.

The stranger cleared his throat. 'Do you want to buy her?' he asked.

Startled, as if the suggestion were somehow improper, my father straightened up, and considered the man properly for the first time. He was wearing an old boiler suit with a shapeless jumper thrown over it, and rubber boots. He had eyes the colour of seawater, a craggy nose which appeared to have been broken in several places, and his face had been so deeply burnt and creased by the sun that it was impossible to tell what age he was – he might have been anywhere between forty and seventy. He took a tobacco tin out of his pocket and began to roll himself a cigarette.

'Is she yours?' my father asked.

The stranger said nothing, but gave an enigmatic nod.

'Don't you want her yourself?'

'You'll be good to her,' the man said, licking the cigarette paper and rolling it up. 'I can see that, and there's nothing for her here. She hasn't been happy since they moved the sheep out of the next field.' He lit his cigarette, pinched a few strands of tobacco off his lower lip and surveyed my father shrewdly through the smoke.

My father's resentment turned to astonishment and delight. A price was quickly agreed and paid. The man fetched a coarse blanket, a bridle and a length of rope from the railway carriage, and showed my father how to fit the bridle. Then he opened the gate and my father led Caroline out of the field and down the lane. As they reached the first bend in the road he turned to wave, but the man had already gone.

'So where is she now?' my mother asked.

'In the meadow.'

A flush was spreading across my mother's face and neck, and her nostrils were pinched together. 'You didn't think of asking me first?' she said.

'I wanted to,' my father said, 'but I couldn't risk it. He might have gone by the time I'd spoken to you and come back. Anyhow, I knew you both liked her, so I didn't think there would be a problem.'

'I see,' my mother said, but her look of displeasure did not soften.

My father looked a little crestfallen. 'Why don't we go and have a look at her?' he suggested at last, and we followed him out into the meadow where we found Caroline tethered to one of the goalpost uprights, head lowered and grazing on the long grass. My mother and I contemplated her for a while without saying anything.

Apparently taking our silence for disapproval, my father launched into a garbled attempt to justify himself, appealing now to sentiment (her sweet nature, her lovely eyes), now to the great cause of natural history (as represented by the school encyclopedia). But he was wasting his time: I was entranced and frankly delighted at the thought of this exotic creature coming to live with us. As for my mother, I think she was angry not so much because he had bought a donkey, but because he had not consulted her first.

'You haven't thought this through at all, have you?' she said.

'No.'

'You don't know anything about keeping donkeys.'

'I can learn,' my father said. 'It'll be fun. And actually, the man I bought her from did give me a few pointers.'

'What did he say?'

'He said, don't put her out to grass in spring, or she'll get laminitis.'

My mother and I considered this gnomic piece of wisdom.

'What's laminitis?' I asked.

'I don't know.'

'Did he tell you anything else?'

'Not that I can remember,' my father said gaily. Then, seeing the strained expression on my mother's face, he said to me, 'Now then, I think what Caroline really needs at the moment is a radish or two. There should be some in the kitchen – I bought a bunch earlier. Why don't you go and see if you can find them?'

I went obediently into the house and started to look for the radishes. It took me a few minutes to find them, concealed as they were under a wilted lettuce in the fruit bowl. When I came outside my parents were conferring in an undertone. They stopped talking when they saw me, and I handed the bunch of radishes to my father. I noticed that the mood had lightened already, and after we had taken turns to feed Caroline the radishes, and my parents had had an absurd and inconclusive argument about whether one should hold a radish by the leaves or by the root when offering it to a donkey, it was clear to me that she would be coming home with us.

The key to my mother's change of heart, I think, was not my father's powers of persuasion, or Caroline's extraordinary charm. It was rather that she saw the donkey as the possible solution to a problem that had been preoccupying her for some time: namely how exactly my father was going to spend his retirement. He himself was not worried in the least. On the contrary, he regarded it as a triumph that he had arranged to retire early – or strictly speaking, to take voluntary redundancy. I don't believe he had thought any further ahead than this; asked what his plans were, he would say he was going to devote himself to 'other interests', or that like a disgraced politician he looked forward to 'spending more time with his family'. These vague aspirations always met with vague approval from his colleagues and acquaintances, but neither bore close analysis, and my mother knew it.

He had no real interests outside work. If anyone had pointed this out to him, he would have denied it indignantly, but it was true. Over the years his private passions, such as they were, had dried up and crumbled away: there were the books on the shelves in the front room, relics of short-lived enthusiasms for such diverse subjects as carp fishing, the life of Napoleon Bonaparte, and watercolour painting, but seldom consulted now; while the pot of more or less indestructible geraniums in the yard was all that remained of a once-keen interest in gardening.

As for spending more time with the family, I would still be out at school all day, so what he really meant was spending more time with my mother. This I think was what she feared. She had no reason not to believe that he would spend his retirement as he currently spent most of his evenings and weekends – collapsed behind the newspaper, or getting under her feet in the kitchen. She had been searching fruitlessly and with growing desperation for a solution to this problem: now, in Caroline, one had presented itself. She might not have expected it to take the form of a donkey, but she was broad-minded enough to recognise it when it appeared – her sole objection was practical.

'How are we going to get her home?' she asked. 'She won't fit in the car. And we can hardly strap her to the roof.'

My father was taken aback – expecting more of a fight, he had prepared himself accordingly, and had not given much thought to questions of logistics. But he only hesitated for a second.

'I'll take another week or so off work and walk home with her,' he announced. This was at once a ridiculous idea, and the simplest and most obvious solution. My mother accepted it without question: such impulsiveness was entirely out of character, and therefore highly promising.

'They can do without me for a bit longer,' my father went on. 'It's not as if we're busy at the moment.' And with that he untied the donkey from the goalpost and took her down to the lake for a walk along the shore. We walked with them across the meadow to the front gate, then stood and watched as they went down the lane side by side, my father walking at the donkey's head with her reins in his hand. At length they disappeared in the shadows under the trees. A big, dusty moon had risen, smouldering above the treetops. The night was so still that we could hear her hooves and his feet crunching on the shingle.

Early the next morning we packed and loaded the hired car, and after breakfast my father prepared Caroline for the journey. He fitted her with the bridle and rope the farmer had given him, and rigged up a kind of harness that allowed him to sling his suitcase on one side of the donkey's back, balanced against a small sack of oats on the other side, with the blanket underneath for padding.

My mother fiddled anxiously with the car keys as we watched him making his final adjustments to the luggage.

'Well,' she said, when everything was ready, 'have a good trip. Let us know if you get stuck.'

'We'll be all right,' my father told her. 'Drive safely. See you in a few days.'

Caroline paid no attention to this exchange, but kept her eyes fixed on the road ahead. They set off, leaving my mother and me to lock the house. We caught up with them on the lake road, before they reached the village. He waved as we drove past, and my mother sounded the horn. Caroline was trotting placidly at his side, as if they had already travelled hundreds of miles together.

As a child, I saw nothing strange in their adventure; now, years later, as I try to imagine what it must have been like, the whole episode seems quite extraordinary. The first part of their journey would have entirely gratified his burgeoning fantasy of himself and Caroline as knights of the road. They followed the single-track road along the lake shore and then turned south. Waterfalls on distant hillsides gleamed where the sun caught them, swallows dipped and flickered across the road ahead, and the musty scent of meadowsweet rose from the ditches. Their route led them through birchwoods, between grassy meadows, in the shadow of towering crags; for several miles they followed the course of a river that thrashed its way over the rocks and tumbled into limpid brown pools, which reminded him of his companion's eyes. In the evenings they would bivouac by the roadside; the donkey tethered, with the blanket thrown over her shoulders (the nights were already turning colder), my father stretched out in his sleeping bag in the lee of the hedge. From the darkness, as he fell asleep, came the noise close by of Caroline's strong jaws tearing and champing steadily at the grass.

But it is the later stages of their journey that intrigue me most, when the fields and woods of the north had been left far behind, and the country lane had become an expressway. I see them picking their way along a hard shoulder strewn with plastic bags, broken glass, hubcaps — the debris of picnics and accidents — and breathing the exhaust fumes of articulated lorries and overloaded minibuses. For my father it was a return to a familiar landscape; for Caroline, the frontier of a different world. But she showed no sign of fear as she crossed it, passing fish farms and allotments, railway sidings and industrial estates, with no more than an occasional sideways look of intelligent curiosity. That night they camped beneath a flyover, and he fed her the last of the oats, while the distant lights of the cranes along the river flashed in the smoky dusk. He could not have guessed then, with the familiar landmarks all round him, that he too was straying into a world that was utterly new and strange.

Our neighbourhood as Caroline first saw it on a dusty August evening: man and donkey made their way slowly down the long, tree-lined street, one of several that ran erratically through the northern suburbs, converging on the city centre. On either side of the road they passed rows of open-fronted shops and canteens, interrupted by the gated entrances to narrow lanes.

It was six-thirty, and the rush hour was ending, but the street was still choked with traffic, and their progress was hampered by the crowds of pedestrians that overflowed the pavements. Caroline's sensitive ears were assailed by the noises of car horns, invective, and the shrieking whistles of the traffic marshals as they attempted to impose order at the intersections. Still she maintained her composure. It was only when they came to the stretch of road that was reserved for the night market, where the traders were putting up their stalls under the trees, unloading crates of bananas and boxes of handbags and video tapes, that her attention was briefly distracted by a bunch of spinach that had fallen into the gutter. But my father pulled at her rope and she followed him patiently into our lane.

During the day, these lanes provided a welcome contrast to the chaos of the street. Except for the noise from outside, which receded as you went further down the alley, the only sound you would hear was the squeal of an unoiled bicycle, or the twittering of the flocks of sparrows that haunted the windowsills. But at this time in the evening, as people returned from work and school, the alley was filled with the usual noises of a residential district – the howling of babies, the squabbling of married couples; children thumping out scales on badly tuned pianos, and the din of television sets and washing machines.

Ours was the last house but one in a three-storey terrace of red and grey brick. They were reasonably spacious, well-built houses, but over the years they had acquired a barnacle-like encrustation of ramshackle balconies, canvas awnings above the windows, air-conditioning units and television aerials, which gave them a cluttered and chaotic look. Each house had a small enclosed yard in front of it. Trees grew in some of these yards, while others had roofs of trellis work with a green canopy of creepers trained over them; higher up, there were window boxes and washing lines that drooped between telegraph poles and the uprights of window frames. On the other side of the lane were the backs of the houses in the next terrace along. In the summer heat all the doors were open, and as they went up the lane, Caroline was afforded glimpses into the domestic life of a dozen households. She took it all in with her moist calculating eyes.

My father had telephoned us most evenings during that week, to reassure us that he and the donkey were still alive and to give sketchy reports of their progress, describing the route they had taken and telling us how many miles they had covered that day. But nothing had prepared us for their appearance when we met them at the front gate. Of course, my father's chin and cheeks were covered by a ragged growth of beard, and he looked as though he had lost a little weight, while the donkey's coat was dusty and streaked with sweat. The musky unwashed smells of man and beast were so mingled that it was hard to tell where one ended and the other began. But the physical effects of the walk could not account, on their own, for the change evident in both of them. My father answered our questions about the journey with a rapt, abstracted look on his face, like a man who has just stumbled out of the cinema.

'What was the weather like?' I asked.

'It was fine.'

'Did you take any photos?'

'You've caught the sun,' my mother said. 'Didn't you find the suncream? I put it in your bag.'

'I didn't see it.'

'It was in the inside pocket.'

'Did you enjoy yourself?'

Caroline had been munching unconcernedly on the pot of geraniums, but when I asked this question she looked sideways at us, so that the whites of her eyes gleamed – hinting, I felt, at great secrets withheld. And my father giggled, and slapped the donkey's rump, as if I had inadvertently referred to a private joke of theirs.

'Yes,' he said, 'we did.'

Naturally the whole neighbourhood knew about Caroline almost before my father had fastened the front gate behind her. It was not that people in the area were particularly fond of gossip, but in such a crowded place it was inevitable that news and rumour travelled fast. By the end of that evening several theories to account for the donkey's arrival were already circulating: my father had bought it thinking it was a racehorse; he was planning to make it into sausages and sell them to the local butcher; it was an ill-judged bribe for a borough councillor; and so on. Each of these theories revealed more about its creator than it did about my father's motives, whatever they might have been.

My father had always been sensitive about what the neighbours might think of him, which had instilled in him a crippling sense of discretion; but he didn't seem to care now about their reaction to Caroline. Maybe he realised that no amount of discretion would hide the fact that he was keeping a donkey in the front yard. And indeed, after they had entertained themselves for a few days with further wild speculation, and the donkey had been formally – and misleadingly – introduced to many of them as 'a family pet', the neighbours no longer took any special notice of her, even when he led her out in the evenings for a walk round the streets.

But perhaps their tolerance was only to be expected. From my bedroom window I could look out over countless back yards, the grey-walled private domains of pigeon-fanciers and radio hams, growers of prize-winning peonies, builders of matchstick models and perpetual motion machines, bigamists and amateur pornographers: in a city of three million restless souls, what was one man's fixation with a small grey donkey?

Unlike the neighbours' yards, which were littered with gas bottles and overgrown shrubs, bicycle parts and bird tables, ours was more or less empty except for the geraniums, which never recovered from the mauling Caroline gave them on her first evening; so there was plenty of room to accommodate a donkey. The outside sink, plugged and filled with water, made an ideal drinking trough. But she still needed a roof over her head – the donkey, my father reminded us, is a hardy and sagacious animal, but ancestrally a creature of the desert margins and as such extremely sensitive to moisture.

Many of my schoolfriends had fathers who were good with their hands, who had workbenches and well-stocked toolboxes and built them bunk beds and go-karts and model farmyards. It had always been something of a disappointment to me that my father showed no interest in this kind of thing. So I was delighted when, the day after he and Caroline returned home, he took me down the road to the builders' merchants, where we bought tools, a drill, nails, screws, some planks and a roll of plastic sheeting with which to build a shelter for the donkey. We had no workbench, but I had the idea of bringing down the desk from my bedroom and using that instead – a suggestion which my father hailed as a stroke of genius. Before we started work, he fetched an apron from the kitchen and put it on. 'Every serious craftsman wears an apron,' he explained. Marvelling at his transformation into a serious craftsman, I held the ends of the planks steady while he knelt on the desk and sawed them into lengths. Once the wooden frame was built we cut pieces of plastic sheeting for the walls and roof and fastened them in place with tacks. The door was made from an old shower curtain, weighted at the bottom with an offcut of wood.

Over the course of the next few weeks, we made more trips to the builders' merchants and replaced this temporary shelter with a more solid but strictly illegal structure of cement blocks, with a stable door split at waist height and a corrugated iron roof. I spent several happy evenings with my father in the yard, mixing cement, holding a spirit level to each new row of blocks he laid to check that it was even, and finally standing on a stepladder holding the sheets of corrugated iron straight as he nailed them to the roof joists.

'Go and get your mother,' he said when the last nail had been driven in. 'I know she'll want to see this. I'll tidy up out here.'

When I came back outside with my mother we found that he had already taken Caroline out of the temporary stable (which he dismantled later that night) and installed her in her new quarters. She poked her head over the door and peered at us quizzically.

'I think she likes it,' he said.

'She's a very lucky animal,' my mother said. 'Is that my apron you're wearing?'

But I was full of admiration for my father and his handiwork. As he stood there in the evening sunshine, with cement in his hair and an apron pocket full of nails, I saw him in a new light, as a man of inner resource and hidden depths, and I wondered what other qualities he might have that were yet to be revealed.

I had never had the opportunity to observe a donkey at close quarters before, and in the weeks after Caroline's arrival I used to take an apple or a handful of potato peelings out to her when I came home from school and study her while she ate them. I wanted to get to know her a little and also to find out, if I could, what it was about her that so appealed to my father. I was struck by her inelegance – the strange combination of strength and delicacy, crudeness and refinement. Like all donkeys, she appeared to have been assembled from a box of spare parts. She had a large, blunt head, with enormously developed jaw muscles; but the features – the nostrils, for instance – were fine and delicate. The upper legs were stocky, but below the knobbly knees they dwindled away, finishing in spindly ankles and incongruously small, neat, black hooves; like a boxer in his boots.

Her coat was coarse and bristly, and called to mind a cheap carpet thrown across her back and flanks. Its colour was predominantly grey, with hints of reddish-brown, silver and charcoal. Her belly, legs and muzzle were cream-coloured. The sparse mane hung straight down, along one side of the neck only; and the stumpy tail, with a few wisps of hair at its end – like a fly whisk, which is what it was – barely reached her knees.

People in those days would often remark on Caroline's benevolent appearance, and it was true that she had a superficial air of mildness and serenity. But this was mainly due to the heavy eyebrows and lashes which concealed her eyes, so that they seemed half-closed, and her shaggy, overhanging eyebrows, reminiscent of a badly thatched cottage. Together they gave her a dreamy expression, as if she had just woken from sleep. The initial impression of gentleness gave way, on closer inspection, to one of mystery, as you tried to look past the long film star's lashes into her great dark eyes, wide open and observant. If she came nearer, perhaps to drink from the trough at your feet, she might look you full in the face, and for a second the eyes could be seen clearly – but their expression was unfathomable.

And so the patient observer was forced to look elsewhere for clues to her character and state of mind. Her ears for instance, which were astonishing not so much for their large size as for their mobility; swinging constantly back and forth in response to sounds, I thought at first. But she was so little concerned by sudden noises around her – a sneeze, a door slamming – that I soon began to wonder if they might not be receiving signals but transmitting them; a key to her thought processes, if only we could read the code.

The way she stood was also enigmatic: front legs slightly splayed, back feet planted one in front of the other, as she browsed over a diminishing pile of hay or a bucket of kitchen scraps. It was a posture of rock-like steadiness, but I noticed that every now and then she would stamp her back foot – not in anger, but in an exploratory way, as if to make sure she still had solid ground beneath her. As if, even on the concrete of our front yard, she could not be completely sure of her footing – fearing that it might crumble away suddenly like scree, or collapse under her, pitching her into the abyss.

But intriguing as they were, none of these observations was enough to explain my father's fascination with Caroline. I would lean on my bedroom windowsill in the evenings and gaze down at her as she rubbed herself against the rough wall of the new stable or peered in through the kitchen window, but the familiar surroundings of our yard only served to emphasise her ordinariness. In the end I decided that whatever it was he saw in her must have been due to the holiday atmosphere, to the spell of the landscape and the long summer evenings – like the gold coins dug out of the fairy hill, which turn to stones on the journey home. And I wondered how long it would be before he tired of her.

We now turn from natural history to the donkey's treatment in literature and an account of glaring inadequacy, beside which Buffon's shortcomings are trivial.

'She was patient, elegant in form, the colour of an ideal mouse, and inimitably small.'

This is Robert Louis Stevenson's description of his companion Modestine, in his Travels with a Donkey in the Cevennes. The entire description - nothing more. And this is the best he can do - the future author of Treasure Island and Dr Jekyll and Mr Hyde - after twelve days on the road, with the donkey constantly by his side? (After twelve days with Caroline, I could have improvised an epic.) And what on earth is an 'ideal mouse' anyway?

The imaginative poverty, the wilful blindness to his subject, is shocking. His savage treatment of the donkey, documented with chilling levity, is a graver fault. Hardly have they left her native village than he is 'incessantly belabouring' the poor beast, and thereafter barely a page goes by without further beatings: 'I promise you, the stick was not idle; I think that every decent step that Modestine took must have cost me at least two emphatic blows.' And having added his own bag to the already heavy burden on the donkey's back: 'I now had an arm free to thrash Modestine, and cruelly I chastised her.'

I highlight these passages not as a case for the animal welfare societies, but rather to throw into relief a further shortcoming, namely the hypocrisy, the excruciating wrong-headedness of Stevenson's judgements about the donkey's character. Consider this: 'Three days had passed, we had shared some misadventures, and my heart was still as cold as a potato towards my beast of burden. She was pretty enough to look at, but then she had given proof of dead stupidity; redeemed indeed by patience, but aggravated by flashes of sorry and ill-judged light-heartedness.'

In other words, Modestine was simply displaying the indomitable character of all donkeys; but her silent resistance to her owner's unreasonable demands is described as 'dead stupidity', while her flashes of spirit are written off as 'sorry and ill-judged light-heartedness.' And when they reach their destination – just after he has sold her, 'saddle and all', for thirty-five francs – he remarks, with infernal presumption, 'As for her, poor soul, she had come to regard me as a god.' No evidence is offered for this – as far as the author is concerned, Modestine's inner life exists only in the realm of fiction, and he is at liberty to invent whatever he likes. (His invention, by the way, is absurd – a dog might worship its master, but long study of their behaviour convinces me that donkeys are strict rationalists.)

Towards the end of the book, there is a lyrical description of a bivouac in a pine wood. The author wakes in the night: 'All around me, the black fir-points stood upright and stock-still.' Just how it was on our first night in the open – not a breath of wind. 'The stars were clear, cold and jewel-like...' Yes – the Milky Way like a shower of diamonds. Ah, memories! But to continue... He sits up and smokes a cigarette, reflecting that 'the outer world, from which we cower into our houses, seemed after all a gentle habitable place; and night after night a man's bed, it seemed, was laid and waiting for him in the fields.' Beautiful – my sentiments exactly. But see what comes next. 'And yet even while I was exulting in my solitude...' Solitude. And the donkey? Only a few feet away, and 'walking round and round at the end of her tether' (as well she might be). But for all practical purposes she is invisible, like some out-of-favour apparatchik painted out of a party photograph. He continues shamelessly: 'I became aware of a strange lack. I wished a companion to lie near me in the starlight, silent and not moving, but ever within touch.' A companion. As if Modestine were merely a walking luggage-rack.

It may seem that I am singling Stevenson out unfairly - there are countless dull-witted brutalisers of animals who have not written so well, or at all. But this is my point: here is a man of great imagination, wit, and almost pathological sensitivity, and yet faced with a donkey, all his powers falter.

Is it too fanciful to suggest that the whole course of Stevenson's later life - his restless wanderings, the journeys to California and the South Seas - was determined here, when he let go of the donkey's halter for the last time? From then on he drifted, anchorless - as if searching for something, without ever being quite sure what it was. This is Stevenson's tragedy: presented at the beginning of his career with a truly noble and worthy subject, he was unable to recognise it as such. When one thinks of what he might have achieved in thi~

5

My father's office was in the heart of the business district, on one of the deep narrow streets that run back from the waterfront. It was a small firm of insurance brokers, with twenty or thirty employees. There was nothing particularly unusual about its appearance; you could have gone into any of the banks and shipping companies and lawyers' offices along the street and found the same wood-panelled corridors, the creaking floorboards and watermarked ceilings, the grimy windows with their views of ventilation shafts and fire escapes. Through a dingy lobby paved with cracked marble tiles, a flight of stairs led to the second floor. Behind the door in the reception hall there was an ancient hatstand, on which the secretaries would hang their umbrellas. A door at the opposite end of the room led to the offices of the various partners and associates. On the wall above the blocked-up fireplace there was a regulator clock in a walnut case with a glass front which displayed its mechanism and the brass pendulum and weights. Mr Low, the managing partner, wound it with some ceremony every week. The clock had little practical purpose, as there was also a digital clock over the door, but it had been there for as long as anyone could remember and served as an unofficial emblem of the company, representing tradition, reliability, punctuality (it still kept excellent time) and similar desirable qualities.

In some ways, though, the hatstand might have made a truer emblem; it had a monumental aspect – testament to the passing of countless jackets and raincoats, hats and umbrellas and their owners, all of which had left no trace on it beyond a slight wearing of the varnish on the hooks. In later years my father often mentioned this hatstand, telling me how he used to contemplate it as his retirement approached and wonder what trace would be left by his own presence in the company apart from the worn patch of carpet under his chair. Was this all he had to show for a life of work? Had he really made this little difference? On the other hand, he had never set out to make a difference, and for a man with little ambition as far as work was concerned his career had been reasonably successful. He had started in the post room straight out of school; he was now a partner, and in between he had worked his way up through most of the positions in the firm.

He did not dislike his work exactly; the details of risk assessments, claims and policy renewals absorbed him from one week to the next, and had become almost interesting as the years passed. Of course, this was partly the effect of the job itself, which inevitably shaped his character; he read small print more carefully, he had grown to like the taste of coffee with powdered milk (for a long time there was no fridge in the office), and he laughed at jokes that he would not have found funny when he first joined the company. Meeting his colleagues for an occasional drink after work, he found himself discussing topics such as motor racing and home improvements with unfeigned enthusiasm.

Still, though, in idle moments at his desk, he had a sensation of faint discomfort, as if there were a draught blowing round his ankles. When he considered his career he could see nothing that he regretted, nothing that looked like a bad decision; and yet he had the feeling that things had not turned out quite as they should have done.

But since Caroline had come to live with us, he was no longer oppressed by thoughts of this kind. Instead, when his attention wandered during a meeting, or as he struggled with a particularly dense report, he found himself wondering what the donkey was doing just then, or what vegetables she might like from the market for her dinner; and the first thing that came to his mind on seeing the hatstand was that he must replace the nails in the stable wall, on which her rope and bridle hung, with proper hooks.

As for Caroline, she may have been comfortably housed, regularly fed, and exercised twice daily with a circuit of the neighbourhood, but when my father was out at work she grew restless. She butted the front door, she gnawed the paint off the kitchen windowsill, and if she heard people coming up the lane she would hang her head over the gate and watch them, snorting and twitching her tail as they went past. But none of these activities provided much consolation, and soon she began to vent her feelings of boredom and loneliness by braying, often for hours at a time. My mother was out most of the day herself, so she was not troubled by the noise, but it was not long before the neighbours started to complain: first of all individually by telephone, and then, one fateful evening, as a delegation.

As it happened, my father was in the yard, watching Caroline while she ate her dinner from an old plastic bucket with no handle. He turned round to find them lined up in front of the gate: pensioners in their pyjamas and dressing gowns, fresh from the bath; harassed-looking men in shirtsleeves, some still holding their briefcases; a mother with a struggling child in her arms. He had known most of them for years – living at such close quarters, within earshot if not full view of each other's private lives, there was little that they did not know about each other.

'We're here about the donkey,' somebody said.

My father waited with interest to see what was coming next. But having assembled so formally in the lane they appeared at a loss how to proceed. Perhaps it was the realisation that they were about to abandon the carefully maintained neighbourly pretence of having seen and heard nothing that made them hesitate. It was an awkward moment; they looked at each other, waiting for someone to speak for all of them. But then the subject of their protest poked her head gravely over the gate and studied them with an air of amused disdain. The child burst into tears, and everyone began to voice their complaints at once.

Faced with this unexpected attack in his own front yard, with Caroline looking on, my father's first reaction was to defend himself vigorously – pointing out to Mrs Young, the neighbour from two doors down, the hypocrisy of lecturing other people on how their donkeys were disturbing the peace, while holding a squalling child in your arms.

'It was the donkey that started him off,' Mrs Young retorted.

'Well, now he's upsetting Caroline,' my father said, 'she's got very sensitive ears.'

At this the donkey launched into a series of shattering brays, which may have proved his point, but also left the neighbours feeling entirely vindicated.

A silence fell. When my father spoke again, his manner was conciliatory. He quite understood their frustration; he was very sorry; he promised to do something. And in fact, he was so quick to offer a solution that I suspected he had been considering it for some time already.

'I'll take her in to work with me,' he announced. 'She only makes all this noise because she gets lonely – this way she can be with me and I can keep an eye on her.'

This was not the outcome the neighbours had been expecting. They had been prepared to stand their ground, to threaten legal action, to insist that he got rid of her. But his meekness had disarmed them – or they may simply have been intrigued to see what his colleagues would think when they encountered the donkey; in any case, they went away mollified.

'Well,' my mother said, when he told us about his plan, 'what will your colleagues think?'

'They'll like her, of course.'

'I meant, what will they think of you?'

'This is a perfectly rational solution,' my father said. 'Although some people in the office may find it eccentric.'

'They'll think you're mad, won't they?'

'All right,' my father said, 'perhaps they will. But that says more about their narrow-mindedness than my behaviour. Anyhow, you know I'm not mad, so that's all that matters.'

I listened to this exchange in silence. Was my father right to be so confident? If my mother did think he was mad, she never said as much to me. Certainly the look she gave him, as we stood there in the yard with the donkey between us, was more admiring than anything else.

'You won't be able to take her on the bus, you know,' she told him.

'I'll ride her, of course. It's not very far, and the exercise will do her good.'

And so, every morning, the two of them would step out of our lane and join the great current of traffic heading towards the city centre. After the first few days, once she had got to know the route and could find the way herself, my father would give Caroline her head and bury himself in the morning paper as he would have done on the bus, his feet nearly brushing the ground. The contents of homes, shops and restaurants spilled out across the pavements, and Caroline picked her way round chairs and tables, washing machines and bicycle parts, rolls of carpet and bolts of cloth and tailors' dummies – paying no attention to the bicycles and mopeds and buses that sped past, inches from her ears.

As they approached the business district, the shops and restaurants gave way to banks and newspaper offices, commodities exchanges and company headquarters with chipped and sooty stone facades, and office blocks in narrow pink brick with metal window frames and balconies of rusty ironwork. The early-morning chill still hung in the shadows between the tall buildings, where at ground level the sun was shut out completely, but when they emerged at intersections the sunlight fell in dazzling patches on the tarmac.

Before going into the office and starting his day's work, my father would lead Caroline across the road to the park on the river embankment. Here, in the shade of the great trees that lined the waterfront, he would remove the saddle (a folded blanket) from her back, rub her shoulders and give her a radish or a handful of runner beans, before leading her back across the road and round the corner to his office.

At the rear of the building there was a small court-yard where, during the working day, Caroline was tethered with a nosebag and a bucket of water. My father's window overlooked it, so he was able to lean out from time to time and check on her, and at lunchtime he would walk down the back stairs and out through the post room to keep her company while he ate his sandwiches. His colleagues indulged him in this, as an eccentricity permissible to a man on the verge of retirement; besides, they were very taken with the donkey. Most days at lunchtime a small crowd would join him outside and pat her back or stroke her ears; or, under my father's watchful eye, they might feed her wholesome scraps from their lunch. They found it invigorating to spend time in the company of this crea-ture whose life was not regulated by the clock, and whose needs and desires were quite different from their own. When she urinated in a steaming arc on the concrete it seemed to them an eloquent demonstration of the fact that the rules they lived by did not apply to her, and as they trooped inside at the end of the lunch hour they felt a pang of envy at the sight of Caroline burying her head deeper in her nosebag, swishing her tail and noisily munching her oats.

But it was not long before she grew fretful in the court-yard, so deep and lightless that it was more like the inside of a chimney. Early one afternoon, when the lunchtime crowd had dispersed, she started bellowing in protest. The enclosed space amplified the noise, until the windows began to rattle in their frames.

After about twenty minutes of this Mr Low, the managing partner, called my father into his office. They stood together for a while by the open window and listened to Caroline tirelessly working her lungs. The noises came with almost mechanical regularity: the creaking inbreaths like a hinge in need of oil, the grating roars of rage and desolation. Mr Low closed the window and turned to my father.

'It's your choice,' he said. 'Either you find alternative transport to work, or somewhere else to keep your donkey. But she can't stay down there.'

'You're quite right,' my father replied. 'It's an intolerable situation. But I do have a suggestion.'

'What's that?'

'Well, there's a lot of space in my office — even more, now that you've moved out . . .'

Until his promotion, when he moved into the managing partner's office with its marble fireplace and a view of the street, Mr Low had shared an office with my father.

'Don't tell me — you want to bring the donkey into the office?'

'Yes.'

'Now listen, Shaw. Don't give me any more reason to doubt your sanity than I have already. It's out of the question. Anyway, how would she be any better off up here than she is in the yard? She needs to be in a field somewhere, surely.'

'What she needs is human company,' my father said. 'She can't stand being on her own.'

'Isn't there someone you could leave her with? Your wife?'

'My wife's very busy – she's working herself. And anyway, I'm not sure how well the two of them get on.'

'A neighbour, then.'

'Oh, I couldn't ask the neighbours. I mean, it's a responsibility – it's not like watering the plants. I really think she'd be happier in here with me.'

Mr Low considered.

'Please,' my father said. 'Just a probationary period. She'll be no trouble, I'm sure of it.'

'All right,' Mr Low said at last, 'if you think it'll keep her quiet, you can try it for the rest of the afternoon. But any more noise and you'll have to take her home. And don't bring her round the front. Use the back door.'

Down in the courtyard, my father did his best to soothe Caroline, picking up the bicycles that she had kicked over in her frustration. Then he led her in at the door that opened off the yard and through the post room, and coaxed her into the service lift. It was just big enough for the two of them together, but only if he sat on her back.

Perhaps wary of the confined space, she refused to go in head first, and he had to get her to back up. Even then she had to turn her head to one side so that the lift doors would close.

When they arrived at the second floor my father rode Caroline out of the lift and slowly along the corridor. At that time in the day, so soon after lunch, a mood of lethargy had settled over the office, but the donkey paused at each open door she came to and stuck her head round it, to the surprise and amusement of her new colleagues, and by the time they reached the end of the corridor the atmosphere was almost lively.

My father's office was a generously proportioned room, with a high ceiling; there was certainly enough space for two people, or for one person and a donkey. His desk stood against one wall, with a pristine square of carpet next to it where Mr Low's desk had been. On the other side of the room there was a photocopier, and by the window a pair of straggling plants that had long since outgrown their pots. From time to time one of them would topple over, scattering damp soil across the carpet.

He installed Caroline in a snug corner near the photocopier, from where she could see everything he was doing, and dragged his desk round so that he sat with his back to the window, facing her. As he had predicted, she gave no more trouble; she nibbled the plants from time to time but apart from this her behaviour was exemplary. And when at the end of the afternoon he drew this fact to Mr Low's attention, and insisted that it was quite impossible to leave the donkey at home, he was told he could bring her back the following day.

Caroline was evidently quite content with this new arrangement. During his lunch break, my father would take her out for a walk along the waterfront, and for the rest of the time she stood quietly in her corner, scratching her rump every now and then against the photocopier's paper tray. Sometimes, when he was grappling with a particularly complex contract, she would come and stand by his chair and look over his shoulder while he read the key clauses out loud to her. 'It helps me to think,' my father told me, 'and as she's in the office I like to keep her informed about what's going on.'

When he was immersed in some dull administrative task, he would relieve the tedium by screwing a piece of scrap paper into a ball and throwing it playfully at the donkey, who would pick it up in her teeth and either deposit it in the waste-paper basket or chew and swallow it thoughtfully. She showed no signs of her previous restlessness, but if my father spent too long on the telephone, Caroline would amble over to his desk and start picking his pencils and biros one by one out of the jar he kept them in and dropping them on the floor. This was the cue for him to wedge the receiver under his ear, open the desk drawer and take out a sugar lump, which he would put on the blotter for her to eat. If he had clients to see, the donkey would be concealed behind a folding screen which he kept propped behind the door for this purpose. 'Our clients are fairly broad-minded,' Mr Low had said, 'but if they see a donkey in your office . . . people leap to all kinds of conclusions, you know. Pot plants, yes, but a donkey – it's the sort of thing that undermines their confidence.'

Of course, the screen did nothing to conceal the creaking of the floorboards as the donkey shifted her weight, or her characteristic smell – a hot, rich, musky odour with an ammoniac undertone, especially towards the end of a warm afternoon. Mr Low need not have worried, though;

no clients were driven away, and Caroline seemed to have a soothing effect on the whole office, like the tank of fish in a dentist's waiting room. And so the working day passed.

The journey home was more leisurely than their journey to work. Freed from professional obligations, they would stop to let Caroline browse on the thin grass of a vacant building plot, or wander down one of the market streets, where she liked to chew the discarded cabbage stumps in the gutters. If the pickings were thin, or she was feeling devilish, she would graze on the potted plants that stood outside so many of the house doors. Nearer home, my father might call in at one of the shops to pick up some groceries for my mother; or they would make circuits of the small park a few blocks from the house, where the couples on the benches and the men playing chess or dominoes at the stone tables under the trees paid them no attention.

When they got home, my father would shut Caroline in the yard and then run upstairs to change his clothes. In the kitchen, he would make tea for himself and my mother, then prepare the donkey's evening bucket of potatoes, carrots and apples and take it out to her.

While she was eating, he might occupy himself by rubbing her down, or sweeping the floor, or making some complex and unnecessary adjustment to her bridle. But when these tasks were finished, he would sit on a hay bale and watch her. He could stay out there for hours, long after the bucket had been emptied – often past our own supper time, until my mother or I would have to go out and fetch him. And as the other concerns that until Caroline's arrival had occupied his evenings – pension plans, my homework, the state of the railways – seemed to lose their urgency, and as he sat in silent communion with the donkey night after night, I began to understand that I had been wrong; he was not going to tire of her.

The notes made by Shaw's father were interspersed with leaflets, occasional papers, photocopied extracts from books and journals, newspaper clippings and abstracts of articles. The following brief selection conveys something of his preoccupations – not to say 'academic interests' – at that time.

Veterinary Neuroscience Quarterly July 1985 (Vol. 12, no. 7)

Sir,

May I add my voice to a debate that has recently been raging in these pages? I refer to the question of the correlation between the physical characteristics of an animal's brain and its intelligence.

Research published in vol. 12 no.5 of this journal identifies the volume of the cerebral cortex as the most accurate measure of an animal's relative intelligence. It comes as no surprise that *Homo sapiens* has the largest cerebral cortex of any species. But the unexpected finding that the domestic donkey, *Equus asinus*, is the only other species with a cerebral cortex of comparable volume to that of a human, has generated a considerable amount of correspondence from your more narrow-minded readers. (See 'Letters' in vol. 12 no. 6.)

Your correspondents insist that the cerebral cortex in equines is largely given over to the control of their motor functions, which are far more complex than those of human beings. However, my own recent, independent research indicates that it is in fact the cerebellum that controls complex motor functions in donkeys, thus freeing the processing power of the cerebral cortex for other activities, such as abstract thought.

Regrettably, I am not in a position to explore the full implications of these findings, as I am currently fighting an appeal against my suspension from the Veterinary Research Council on charges of professional misconduct. Any contributions that your readers may feel moved to make towards my fighting fund and to my ongoing research activities would be most welcome.

Yours, etc.

'Dr Synapse'

is a process that may take many years. But what is the aim of our exercises? Where does the training stop? Many people assume that the riding master's work is done when the horse has learnt to obey commands: when we ask it to trot, it trots; when we ask it to gallop, it gallops; when we ask it to jump a fence, it jumps the fence. And according to the orthodox view, the education of the horse involves a progression from basic footwork to exercises of greater complexity and difficulty, culminating in manoeuvres which most sober people would refuse to believe possible unless they had seen them performed – such as the double somersault, with the rider sitting bolt upright in the saddle throughout, which Steinbrecht demonstrated at the Spanish Riding School in 1882.

But this is a misconception. These manoeuvres, useful or impressive though they might be, are not an end in themselves, but rather a means of developing and strengthening the bond between man and beast. As Steinbrecht once put it, 'The ultimate goal of all our efforts is to bring about a state of perfect unity between horse and rider.' This is well illustrated by the experience of a Galician captain of hussars, who went on campaign with an intelligent and well-trained bay mare. After several weeks in the field, he found that he no longer had to command his horse. No sooner had he thought of a manoeuvre than the horse was carrying it out, without having been asked. And on more than one occasion towards the end of the campaign, the horse seemed actually to have anticipated his thoughts – he would find her breaking into a trot, for example, or fording a river at a certain point, and only then realise that this was exactly what he wanted her to do.

There is also the account of one of Marshal Ney's dragoons on the retreat from Moscow: having had two horses shot under him at Borodino, and after losing one to wolves and another to frostbite, he found a donkey abandoned in a barn and rode it for 800 miles – across ice-bound rivers, through the Russian lines – without bridle, reins or directions. 'Never,' he told Ney afterwards, 'have I had such an understanding with any animal as I did with that donkey.' According to

FORTHCOMING PUBLICATIONS

Mindfulness in the Saddle: A Book of Alternative Dressage by Cathy Sodergren, Ph.D

This pioneering study offers a comprehensive introduction to the theory and practice of Alternative Dressage by one of its leading exponents. Cathy Sodergren makes a passionate case for abandoning the restrictive and damaging practices of classical dressage in favour of more radical and holistic methods, with the aim of establishing a direct, elemental connection between horse and rider.

Using techniques drawn from a range of sources including Native American shamanistic traditions, the Eleusinian Mysteries and the philosophy of the Golden Mean, she shows how the barriers between horse and rider can be overcome in a moment of intense and joyous spiritual awakening.

Cathy Sodergren has been developing the principles of Alternative Dressage since the early 1970s at her stable in southern California where she lives, rides and works as a veterinarian and equine therapy facilitator. She is the author of *Your Horse Has a Third Eye Too* and *Riding Beyond the Ego*.

'Reading Dr Sodergren's book with my Lippizaner mare, Maya, was a profoundly enriching experience for both of us.'

– Elliot Pappenhacker, Professor of Equine Behavioral Science at the University of Western Colorado and author of *We Are All Mammals, Aren't We?*

6

In the city's unforgiving climate, with its extremes of temper-
ature and its damp air laced with exhaust fumes, Caroline's
stable soon took on a weathered and shabby look. After a
few months its corrugated iron roof was streaked with rust
and its walls were blackening, and it looked at least as old as
the house and the yard in which it stood. I grew accustomed
to Caroline's presence inside the stable as well, and soon the
wisps of straw that blew about the yard and the pervading
smell of hay and ammonia were as unremarkable to me as
the gas bottles and the dustbin. But everything about the
donkey exerted a powerful fascination for the classmates
and acquaintances who would come home with me to see
her after school.

To them she was still a novelty; there were no other
donkeys in the neighbourhood, after all, and I suppose
her small size and her homely appearance made her

approachable. My father of course took their interest as a tribute to Caroline's personality, and was only too happy to have them as an audience when he was feeding her or sweeping out the stable. They would cluster excitedly round the stable door, gingerly touching her nose, competing to feed her handfuls of grass or commenting admiringly on the length of her ears. Meanwhile I looked on with the air of one who has seen it all before, answering their questions and displaying my knowledge of donkey-related matters. 'Laminitis,' I would say, 'you haven't heard of it? It's a disease of the feet.'

One evening the visitor was my friend Arthur, a thin boy from my maths class whose reputation as an intellectual was based on the steel-rimmed glasses that he occasionally wore and his apparently genuine passion for linear equations. The donkey submitted patiently to being led up and down the lane, and later Arthur offered her gingerly, on outstretched palms, an apple that my father had cut up for him. Then we went inside to eat boiling sausage with potato salad.

My father was the first to finish eating. He always ate quickly these days, in his haste to get back to the stable. 'May I get down, please?' he would ask with exaggerated politeness, playing the part of the overgrown child, and my mother would roll her eyes and ask what he could be doing out there that was so fascinating. But today she told him he was setting a bad example, and he should wait until every-one else had finished. It would not have crossed my father's mind to disobey her. He stayed where he was, stirring fret-fully in his chair, watching us eat.

'There's still some left,' my mother said mercilessly when the plates were empty, 'can anyone finish it up? No? A skinny boy like you,' she told Arthur, 'you should be eating more.'

'I'll take it for lunch tomorrow,' my father said quickly, getting up and collecting our plates. He bowed to Arthur and me, kissed my mother noisily on the cheek, put the plates down by the sink and went out.

After Arthur and I had helped my mother with the washing up, I was slightly at a loss as to what we should do. It was Arthur who suggested a game of chess. My admission that I hadn't played before, which I thought might put him off, only made him more keen on the idea and he promised to teach me the rules.

I felt sure there was a chess set in my bedroom cupboard, but if it had ever been there, it wasn't there now. My mother had no idea where it might be either, and after we had turned out the cupboards in the living room, Arthur and I went outside to ask my father. I didn't really expect him to know where it was, but I was glad of the excuse to show Arthur the donkey again. We were like theatregoers after the performance, drawn by the irresistible magnetism of the stage door.

I knocked at the door of the stable, and then, hearing no answer, pulled it open.

And there, on an upturned bucket, in the dim light of a sixty-watt bulb, was the chessboard, with my father sitting on a bale of straw on one side and Caroline facing him on the other. My father glanced up as we opened the door, but hardly registered us; he cast his eyes down again and I could see he was considering the state of play. Caroline was standing with her neck craned forward and her ears pulled back, moving her head from side to side as if she were studying the board as well. They were both leaning so far forward that I expected them to bump heads at any moment.

At length my father moved a piece and sat up, watching Caroline expectantly. The donkey's nostrils twitched, but she did not raise her eyes from the board; she had not looked up even when we came in, and I realised she had powers of concentration that my father could not match. Drawing back her lips to expose her formidable teeth, she lowered her head, picked up one of the pieces delicately between her incisors and moved it down the board.

I was astonished and impressed by her dexterity; I had been half-expecting her to knock all the pieces over. But now my father made another move, and again Caroline bent over the board as if considering, picked up another of her pieces and moved it in the same way. This was repeated several times, and finally it dawned on me that they were actually playing a game.

I glanced at Arthur to see how he was reacting to this amazing spectacle, then nudged him. He frowned and pursed his lips; I could see that he was concentrating on the game. 'Your father's in trouble,' he said.

I was irritated by his reaction; I felt he was making a conscious effort not to be impressed. But he was right – from the way my father sighed as he contemplated the board after Caroline had made a move, it appeared that the donkey had the upper hand. The end came quite suddenly; my father knocked over his king in resignation and Caroline cocked her ears and tossed her head, her eyes glinting with triumph.

'She plays to win,' Arthur said, and now he looked impressed.

We inspected the final position. It meant little enough to me, but my father explained proudly how Caroline had outflanked him from the left with her rook, before driving her queen straight through his ragged line of pawns. 'That's three games in a row now,' he said. 'She's such an aggressive player, you see; I'm on the back foot the whole time, and eventually I crumble. But elegant as well – there's nothing brutish about Caroline's game. Just a devastating combination of strength and grace . . . Did you boys want something?'

'Actually,' I said, 'we were looking for the chess set – but I suppose we could play draughts instead.'

'No, no,' said my father. 'Why don't you join us? We can have a little tournament.'

So we pulled up a couple more bales of straw to sit on, and Arthur set up the board while my father explained the rules. After a few trial games he decided I was ready to challenge Caroline, and Arthur and I took turns to play against her.

As a complete novice, I was not surprised when the donkey beat me, although I had no way of telling how good a player she really was. Her interpretation of the rules did seem a little unorthodox; every now and then my father would pick up a piece she had just put down and move it to another square, remarking, 'An interesting move, Caroline, but remember we're not playing fairy chess today,' or, 'That gambit would have rattled a grand master, but let's keep things simple for the boys.' Caroline would watch these interventions suspiciously, with her head on one side. It may have been significant that Arthur lost to her twice, and described her as 'a formidable opponent'; but again, I was in no position to judge how good Arthur was either.

The exhilarating novelty of playing chess with a donkey more than made up for the successive defeats, and Caroline was positively skittish when we finished; she butted Arthur playfully in the back as he was returning the chess pieces – marked faintly with the imprint of her teeth – to their box.

We dragged the hay bales back into place and spent a soothing ten minutes stroking Caroline's nose and feeding her carrots. 'For humans, carrots are a source of vitamin A, which is good for the eyes, as you boys probably know,' my father remarked, 'but in donkeys, carrots act directly on the cerebral cortex. These things are pure brain food – any root vegetables are, but carrots are best.'

Later that evening, after Arthur had gone home, I finally put to my father the day's most burning question: what had possessed him to try combining a donkey and a chess-board?

'Well, the vet came round the other day to give her a tetanus shot,' my father said, 'and he told me she needed something to occupy her brain. Donkeys are highly intelligent creatures, you know – if you leave them on their own with nothing to do they get fractious. We all need challenges, and Caroline is no exception.'

'So the vet told you to play chess with her?' my mother asked.

'Not in so many words,' my father admitted, 'but it seemed like the obvious choice to me. We were in the park last week and we passed some people playing chess, and I went over to speak to someone I knew, and while we were talking, all the time Caroline was watching the game. She was completely engrossed, in fact – I couldn't get her to come away until they'd finished.'

I wanted to know how easy it had been to teach her.

'Once I'd set the board up and gone through the basic moves a few times, she soon got the hang of it,' my father said. 'The rules are simple enough, after all – a child could learn them.

'Although I must say,' he went on, 'I think Caroline picked it up a little more quickly than you did. She's a natural. As for that boy Arthur, trying to castle with a bishop – she could teach him a thing or two as well.'

While sceptics might find the notion of a donkey playing chess difficult to believe, no one would deny that Caroline was physically capable of moving the pieces, and having conceded that, the only thing really in dispute is the quality of her game. My mother was no chess player, but I think she saw straight away what I only understood afterwards, that ultimately the standard of play was irrelevant; my father's matches with the donkey were the vehicle for the pure intercourse of two minds. I picture the stable on a winter evening, the two of them bent over the board, the unshaded light bulb throwing strange shadows across the walls; or with the door wedged open in the soft rain of early summer – utterly absorbed in their game, oblivious to the water gushing over the roof and gurgling in the drain holes – and my mind turns to the bare cells to which medieval anchorites retreated when they wanted to be alone with their visions.

Of the hundreds, if not thousands of games so far played by Caroline, only a tiny proportion have been recorded, because her opponents were generally unwilling to write down their moves if she did not, feeling I suppose that it put them at a disadvantage. I did make notes of a few of the games that we played together, but they tend to be short and one-sided, and thus of little interest to the general reader. Occasionally, though, at the beginning of her career, I would record a game of hers against a promising local player, and it is one of these that I present below.

In a bold piece of attacking play, Black gains control of the centre using only her Knights, then sacrifices both of them in order to capture White's Queen. The reliance on Knights is characteristic, and I can only assume that Caroline felt an affinity with these pieces on account of their appearance. Playing the game over again, I found one or two surprising moves, which may be due to inaccurate transcription - at the time I had not completely mastered algebraic notation and I sometimes made mistakes.

White - Unknown. Black - Caroline.

1. b4 e5

2. Bb2

White shows the influence of the hypermodern school, playing Tartakower's Orangutan Opening* and then fianchettoing his Bishop on the Queen's side.

Nc6

3. Nf3 Bc5

Black counters with the Classical Defence, a favourite response of hers when faced with the Ruy Lopez as well.

4. d4 d5

5. dxc5 Nf6

6. e4 0-0

7. exd5 Nxd5

8. Bd3

Better might be Bc4 or Bxe5. White is in danger of becoming boxed in.

      b6

9. 0-0 bxc5

10. Qd2 Rb8!

Protecting the flank by pinning White's Pawn at b4.

11. Re1 Nf4

12. Be4 Nd4!

Black's Knights take up a strong position in the centre.

13. Nxe5 Qg5

14. h4 Qh5

15. Re3

More useful would be c3, threatening Black's Knight.

      Nde2+

16. Qxe2

A bad error. For now:

      Nxe2+

17. Rxe2 Qxe2

and White's position is considerably weakened.

18. Bd3 Qd1+

19. Kh2 Rxb4

20. Nc3

But White will have little chance to develop this attack.

      Qh5

21. Ba3 Qxe5+!

A brilliantly economical move!

22. f4 Qxf4+

23. g3

White is completely lost.

Qf2+

24. Kh1 Rxh4+

25. gxh4 Bh3

26. Bh1

Ineffectual. Rg1 is the only move likely to be of any use to White at
this point.

hxf1

27. Ne4

Another blunder. For now:

Qg2 mate.

*First documented in the New York tournament of 1924. In the version
of the story that I first heard, Tartakower, finding himself with an afternoon
to spare between games, visited the Bronx Zoo, took a fancy to an orangutan
there, and played several games of chess with her. This was her first move
in a particularly elegant attacking game which she went on to win comfortably.

According to another version, however, while Tartakower did indeed visit
the zoo and admire the orangutan, they did not, so far as we know, actually
play chess together. Instead, Tartakower simply announced (to the zookeeper?
to the tournament officials?) that he would dedicate his next game to her.

Whichever version of the story is true, the following day he opened
with 1. b4 and although he subsequently lost the game, this move has been
known as the 'Orangutan Opening' ever since.

The arrival of Caroline had come as an immense relief for my mother in many ways. My father always used to return from work exhausted, and incapable of devoting his full attention to anything; he would answer questions absently, part of his mind still fixed on the details of a partners' meeting or a loss adjuster's report. But at the end of a day in the office with Caroline he was positively light-hearted and would wander in and out of the kitchen as he prepared the donkey's evening meal, chattering incessantly: ideas for where we might take her on holiday next summer, or his plans for the allotment he hoped to secure (a man who for years had shown no interest whatsoever in gardening), to be turned over to the intensive and scientific cultivation of brassicas, root crops, alfalfa and clover as fodder for the donkey, in deep beds, fertilised with her own dung. Meanwhile at one end of the kitchen table my mother filled vol-au-vent cases for an office party and at the other I pretended to concentrate on my homework, although I was actually indulging in a rich daydream of Sunday afternoons at the allotment: I saw my mother and myself in deckchairs, sharing a flask of tea, and my father knee-deep in dung and vegetables, hoeing in a scientific manner, while Caroline stood beside him wearing an old straw hat, with holes cut in the crown for her ears, to shade her eyes from the sun.

My mother did not mind that his conversation now consisted almost entirely of variations on a single theme; she was happy to share the front yard and sometimes the kitchen too with a donkey. For thanks to Caroline her husband had been restored to her – the impetuous, carefree figure she dimly remembered from the early days of their marriage.

But in the weeks after our first tournament in the stable, my father took to playing chess with the donkey every night, often until quite late; Caroline, the results suggested, was one of those thinkers whose brains are at their most agile in the small hours. Perhaps he felt guilty about neglecting my mother – or he may simply have felt that their increasingly one-sided chess games were no longer providing the donkey with enough of an intellectual challenge. In any case, one evening he made the following proposal.

'How would it be,' he said to my mother with studied carelessness, 'if Caroline went in to the office instead of me? That way I could spend the whole day with you at home, if you liked.'

'But who will do your job if you're here all day?' my mother asked.

'Caroline will, of course. If she can play chess she can certainly learn to analyse a policy document and calculate a premium – and I'm sure Mr Low can find plenty of other things for her to do. A mind like hers would be an asset to any company.'

It took my mother a few seconds to absorb this suggestion.

'I know Caroline is intelligent,' she said carefully, 'but that's not the point – do you seriously think a donkey can do a man's job in an office? She won't be able to answer the telephone for one thing. And what's she going to do when there's a meeting?'

But my father was perfectly serious. Whether it was the exceptional abilities of the donkey that convinced him, or his low opinion of the work involved, he was sincere in his belief that Caroline could carry out his duties as well as he could.

'I've thought it all through,' he told us. 'The receptionist will deal with all the phone calls. And as for the departmental meetings, they're only once a week, and I can represent Caroline in those – I'd want to go in from time to time anyway, just to show my face and keep an eye on things.' What was more, he revealed, the managing partner had already approved the idea. 'She's very popular with my colleagues, you know; they're used to her now and they all like her, and that's really the most important thing in this line of work, to be part of the team. Her interpersonal skills are exceptional – she's far better with people than some of my partners.'

I think my mother was still far from convinced by this

reasoning, but she did not object any further: if his colleagues were prepared, for whatever reason, to indulge him, she was not about to complain.

Caroline quickly settled into a working routine. At seven each morning my father would get up and go down to the kitchen to chop a couple of apples for her breakfast bucket, which he now supplemented with some oats or a cup of molasses – 'to feed her brain', as he explained. At seven twenty he would take this nourishing mixture out to the stable and put some hay in the rack for her. While the donkey was eating, he would groom her with a stiff brush. At seven forty-five Caroline would leave for the office, ambling down the lane while my father stood at the gate and waved her off, like a caricature of the dutiful wife. At seven fifty he would go back to the kitchen and prepare breakfast for himself and my mother: toast and strong tea, which he carried up to the bedroom on a tray. The donkey returned in the early evening, to be welcomed with an apple or a handful of raisins. Then there would be further careful brushing, an inspection of her hooves, and another solid meal, followed by a walk round the park or a game of chess.

Needless to say, I was extremely curious about what exactly Caroline did in the intervening eight hours in the office, but I never succeeded in establishing this with any certainty. Perhaps my mother's suspicions were correct, and she simply spent the days standing in her usual place, dragging her heels down the skirting board, while the letters and faxes piled up unanswered on my father's empty desk. But the reactions of his colleagues suggested that the donkey was making more profitable use of her time than my mother feared. Once a week, usually on Wednesdays, he would ride Caroline into the office in order to attend the partners' meeting and to discuss the donkey's professional development. My mother had assumed that this day in the office would be spent undoing all the damage Caroline had done during the previous week. But according to my father this was not the case: the managing partner believed she was making a valuable contribution. Morale had never been so high, and the firm had met all its performance targets for the last quarter, an achievement which he put down to Caroline's influence. This positive view was shared by nearly everyone else. The finance director spoke with admiration of her head for figures; Human Resources praised her dedication, and the secretaries said she had a lovely personality.

The only person who did not get on with Caroline, it turned out, was Miss Lamb, the receptionist, whose workload had increased as a result of having to deal with all the phone calls that my father would previously have taken. But this did not trouble her so much as their working relationship.

'There's just something abrasive about her manner,' Miss Lamb had told him. 'Some female executives are like that. She's probably all right with you, of course, you're a man. But I find it very undermining.'

Caroline would, for example, wait until my father was out of the office before kicking over her empty water bucket, so that Miss Lamb had to go in and fill it for her.

'It's not in my job description,' Miss Lamb said. 'We're all supposed to get our own drinks here. Even Mr Low wouldn't ask me to make coffee for him. And the other day she kicked over her bucket just after I'd filled it. I had to get down on my hands and knees and mop it up with a couple of tea towels from the kitchen. And she just looked at me like this, right down the length of her nose, as if it was my fault.'

Of course, Miss Lamb added hastily, there was no denying Caroline's commitment to the firm, but she had much preferred working with my father.

Despite these frictions, and the mystery surrounding how Caroline spent her time, these few months were arguably the most satisfying of my father's professional life. The fact that they were the last months before his retirement, and that he spent hardly any of that time in the office, might be taken as a poor reflection on his whole career up to this point – but he was in such high spirits that none of this mattered to him at all.

Mr Low had taken my father by surprise by announcing that he would be happy to extend the donkey's contract for as long as she wanted. 'Just because you're calling it a day,' he said, 'you shouldn't feel that Caroline has to go too.'

My father was startled. Did they seriously think he would go on sending Caroline out to work when she could be enjoying her retirement with him at home? He did not entirely trust Mr Low either; after all, the offer seemed to imply that his colleagues thought more highly of the donkey than they did of him. But there was nothing in the managing partner's manner to indicate that an insult had been intended, and my father confined himself to a polite refusal, explaining that he was worried about the tax implications if the donkey continued in paid employment after he had stopped working himself. And so it was agreed that the two of them should leave at the same time.

The firm's custom, when an employee retired, was for everyone to have lunch at the City Garden, a restaurant in the street behind the office which was generally agreed to have the finest kitchen in the area. My father had been looking forward to this – it was the season for crayfish, the restaurant's speciality; boiled to a dusky red, glistening with oil and flecked with chopped garlic and chillies, it was a favourite of his. But on the day of the party, after Mr Low had locked the office and the staff had gathered in the courtyard, they led him not round the corner to the City Garden but in the opposite direction, towards the waterfront.

'We felt the atmosphere at the City Garden wouldn't really be to Caroline's taste,' Mr Low explained, 'so we've made an alternative arrangement.'

They crossed the road and went into the park on the river embankment, where my father had so often rubbed Caroline down in the mornings. It was little more than a strip of grass, sandwiched between the road and the water's edge. A thin straggling hedge screened it from sight of the traffic, if not from the noise and fumes, and it was completely overshadowed by a row of massive spreading trees whose branches dipped on one side towards their reflections in the water and stretched out on the other to brush the windows of the buildings across the street. Under the trees a long trestle table had been set up on the grass and laid for lunch.

'What's this?'

'We're having a picnic. Come and sit down.'

It turned out that the 'picnic' had been ordered from the City Garden, so my father would have his crayfish after all; there were bottles of beer and lemonade cooling in buckets of ice and water under a tree, and a tub of water and a dish of cold starters for Caroline.

While his colleagues were milling about, enjoying a drink and the novelty of being away from their desks, and finding their places, Mr Low took my father's arm and led him towards his seat. It was usual, at lunches like this, for the retiring member of the firm to be given the place of honour; so my father was surprised, as Mr Low led him past the head of the table, to see there was no chair for him. As he pondered the meaning of this, he caught his foot against something; it was a metal peg that had been driven into the ground.

'Ah, yes,' said Mr Low, as my father pulled his shoe off and clutched his sore toes, 'I expect you're wondering – well, we thought it might be fun to put Caroline here.'

My father said nothing, but went on massaging his toes.

'You're not happy?'

'It's not on my account,' my father mumbled, cramming his shoe back onto his foot, 'but putting a donkey at the head of the table – I just think it's disrespectful to you.'

'Nonsense,' said Mr Low. 'It's not the head of the table. Just think of it as the end – and I'll be sitting at the other end anyhow.' He led my father a little way down the far side of the table and pulled out a chair for him.

Caroline, meanwhile, had been patiently waiting under the tree where the drinks were chilling, nibbling experimentally at the foliage above her head and dipping her muzzle in the nearest bucket of ice and water. 'No,' said Mr Low, 'don't get up – allow me.' He went and picked up the end of the donkey's rope where it trailed in the grass and, with a mixture of gallantry and fumbling excitement, as if he were helping a young woman off with her coat, led her to the head of the table and tethered her to the peg.

When the crayfish had been dismantled and consumed and their remains scattered across the table, and the beer bottles were empty, and the conversation had grown raucous and incoherent, Mr Low banged on the table for silence and rose to his feet.

'We're here today,' he said, 'as you all know, to say good-bye to a colleague who's made a valuable contribution – a unique contribution – to this company.'

My father lowered his eyes modestly.

'A colleague whose energy and dedication are exemplary. Who understands the importance of hard work. Who is respected by colleagues and clients alike – and not forgetting, of course, that wicked sense of humour.'

Everyone chuckled appreciatively, and my father took a bashful sip at his empty glass.

'A dear colleague, who's now embarking on a well-deserved retirement, and who I know we're all going to miss very much indeed.

'So I'm sure you'll all want to join me now in raising a glass to Caroline, and wishing her a long and happy retirement.'

The toast was drunk with cheers, applause and clinking of glasses. As Mr Low sat down, everyone turned to see how the donkey had taken the speech. Fully aware that she was the centre of attention, Caroline looked up from her dish of starters and cast a supercilious eye over the assembled company. Then she tossed her head, snorted, and kicked over a chair.

Everyone took this as a signal that the proceedings were closed. They stood up, wiping their hands ineffectually on the tablecloth, and shook hands with my father. Then, their inhibitions washed away by several glasses of beer, they all rushed to the head of the table, jockeying to have their pictures taken with Caroline.

My father stayed rooted in his seat, his pride that the

donkey's achievements had been recognised mingled with a stronger and growing feeling that somewhere in the afternoon's events, or perhaps over the last few months, there had been a disastrous mistake. But before he had managed to work things out to his satisfaction he was distracted by Mr Low, who called my father down to his end of the table.

'I hope I didn't go on for too long,' Mr Low said. 'I'm afraid I got a little carried away – we're just so grateful for everything she's done for us. And we're grateful to you, of course,' he went on hurriedly. 'In fact, we wanted to give you this.'

He felt in the plastic shopping bag at his feet and brought out a small parcel, which he presented to my father. 'Just a small token of our appreciation for your long service.'

My father turned the parcel over uncertainly in his hands.

'Go on, open it.'

It was a leather pouch, with my father's initials embossed in gold on the flap.

'It's to keep your tees in,' said Mr Low. 'You wear it on your belt when you're out on the golf course – look, there's a loop on the back.'

'But I don't play golf,' said my father in consternation.

'You don't? I knew it – I told them, bowls is your game, isn't it?'

'Chess.'

'Of course, chess.' He sighed, then went on: 'Still, you don't have to keep tees in it, do you? You could use it for, er – you know, as a wallet or something. Anyhow, there it is, with our best wishes.'

'Thank you.'

There was a shriek of laughter from the other end of the table; Caroline was eating the flowers off Miss Lamb's straw hat.

'Naturally,' Mr Low continued, clearing his throat, 'we have something for Caroline as well, but unfortunately we can't present it to her today.'

'That's all right,' said my father, 'there's really no need . . .'

'It'll be delivered to your house – I hope that's acceptable.'

'Of course,' my father said. 'As you like – excuse me.' Further shrieks could be heard from the end of the table; the donkey had finished the flowers, and started on Miss Lamb's hat.

My father pushed his way into the throng and prised the uneaten fragments of the hat from Caroline's jaws. Then he climbed onto her back, shook hands all round and rode away, followed by a crowd of tipsy and excited well-wishers. When they reached the park gate everyone stopped and applauded as the two of them went through the gate and out onto the pavement. Someone had stuck a wreath of plaited grass over the donkey's ears. Either the hat, or the flowers, or the cold starters had not agreed with her, and she suffered from stomach cramps all the way home.

A few days later, Caroline's present was delivered by courier; a large cardboard box bound at the seams with parcel tape. Inside, in a nest of shredded newspaper, lay the regulator clock from the office reception.

PERFORMANCE APPRAISAL FORM

Name:	Position:	Length of service:
Caroline	Managed accounts executive	8 months
Ref:	Appraisal date:	Appraiser:
04/5263	12 April	CY Low

Description of current role and duties:

Dealing with renewals and amendments to clients' policies, collecting premiums, processing accounts, risk assessment, dealing with paperwork and records.

Alignment with company values:

It would not be an exaggeration to say that Caroline embodies our company values of discretion, integrity and dependability.

Appraiser's comments:

Caroline's work rate is formidable, and she has the gift of remaining calm under pressure. She always pulls her weight in her team and shows leadership potential. As for her personal image, she is always well-groomed and never over-dressed.

She has made an important contribution to the company in the short time she has been working here, and we hope she will give some serious consideration to the possibility of a long-term future with us. We would like to see her expanding her current brief to include marketing, business development and presentations to clients, in preparation for a future management role. Of course, like many of us, she has to balance the demands of work and family, but it would be a pity if she sacrificed a promising career purely for the sake of her domestic commitments.

Short-term development and training objectives:

It was decided that Caroline should attend workshops on personnel management and an introductory course on actuarial science in order to round out her core skills.

Career development – medium to long term goals:

No specific ambitions were expressed, but the appraiser made it clear that an application for a management vacancy in 1 to 2 years' time would be looked on favourably.

Signed (Appraisee):	Signed (Appraiser):	Date:
F Lamb pp. Caroline	LYL	12/4

8

My father was not greatly affected, outwardly at least, by the series of humiliations he had endured at his retirement party. Perhaps he felt that since his career had meant so little to him, there was no sense in being upset by the unsatisfactory way in which it had ended. He fixed a bracket to the stable wall and hung the donkey's new clock on it, next to her nosebag and brush.

But on the first evening of his retirement, after Caroline had been shut in for the night and I had gone to bed, he held a celebration of his own. He collected all his ties from the chest of drawers in his and my mother's bedroom and took them out to the yard. Then he built a small pyre from crumpled sheets of newspaper and arranged the ties on top. Finally he doused the whole edifice with the bottle of brandy that he had won in an office raffle some years earlier, lit a match and set fire to it.

The smell of burning drew me to my bedroom window just in time to see him taking off the tie he was still wearing and tossing it onto the pyre. My mother was out there with him and he stepped back, took her hand and together they watched in silence as the ties were consumed by the flames. I had an urge to cheer, or to applaud, but I sensed that to do so would be to intrude on a private ceremony. The fire burnt quickly; when the blaze went out my father heaved a deep sigh of relief, my mother squeezed his hand and smiled at him, and they went back inside, leaving behind a heap of smoking ashes on the concrete.

It did occur to me afterwards that his colleagues' effusive praise for Caroline's work, and the way they allowed her to upstage my father so completely at the party, might have been deliberate, a way of getting back at him for introducing a donkey into the office and for neglecting his professional duty for weeks at a time – but this would have been to assume a degree of subtlety on their part, not to mention a sense of humour, which they did not possess. In any case, their affection for the donkey was not feigned; they would come to our house to see her on the pretext of consulting my father about some work-related matter that could just as easily have been discussed over the phone. They would sit out in the yard drinking tea and talking about risk analysis, while Caroline hung her head over the stable door and watched them, until she got bored and began snorting and breathing damply down my father's neck.

'I'm sorry,' he would say, 'but Caroline doesn't like people talking shop these days.'

With relief the visitor would change the subject from insurance to donkeys, and my father would lean back in his chair, reaching behind him to pat Caroline's muzzle, and suggest a walk round the park.

His home life, to begin with at least, was modest and uneventful. If my mother was putting an order together, he and Caroline would make themselves useful in the kitchen – he might grease a baking sheet, and Caroline would stir the mixture for a batch of scones with a wooden spoon clamped between her teeth, while simultaneously cracking walnuts for a cake by trampling them delicately under her back hooves.

If my mother had no work and the weather was fine, they might go out for the day. My father would be up early, preparing a picnic, while I ate my breakfast. By chance or otherwise these expeditions of theirs always took place on school days, so I was never invited. They would leave as I was setting off for school, my mother mounted on the donkey, with the picnic rug beneath her and the basket balanced across her knees, while my father held the reins. In those days, an hour's walk from our house brought you to the outer edge of the city; they would wander off into the countryside, among orchards and fields and ditches, along dusty roads lined with poplars. As the sun climbed higher they would find some shady place, tether the donkey, and spread the picnic rug out on the grass. Towards evening they would retrace their steps, or wait at one of the country stations for the hourly train that threaded its way lazily back through the suburbs, depositing them at last from an almost-empty carriage into the rush-hour traffic at the end of our road.

My parents would return from these excursions in a happy stupor, which was only partly explained by the strength of the sun and the bottle of wine my father had put in the picnic basket. They walked up our lane hand in hand, with wisps of dry grass stuck to their backs, while the donkey stumped patiently along behind them. And I remember one afternoon returning from school and coming into the kitchen to find my father sitting on my mother's knee, wearing one of her hats, and kissing her with an enthusiasm I had never seen before. Meanwhile Caroline was standing by the gas hob, on which a saucepan was simmering, looking ready to lift the lid if it boiled over, and watching them with her usual air of dreamy benevolence.

The renewed passion in my parents' relationship was unmistakable, but I often wondered about the precise nature of my father's obsession with Caroline. At first it had been possible to see her as the neighbours did, a harmless if incomprehensible fixation, the equivalent of the model railway in the attic or the stamp collection. The donkey herself had seemed of minor importance; she was the framework on which to hang such absorbing occupations as the construction of a stable, research into questions of diet and ailments, the daily walk, and the adjustment of bridles. But by now it should have been clear even to the meanest intelligence that she meant more to him than this.

Had it been love at first sight? Maybe at their first meeting he had caught some signal – a twitch of the ears, an unguarded stare – which my mother and I had not noticed, but which spoke to him unmistakably of their destiny together. Or had it crept up on him slowly, as bit by bit the enormous power and subtlety of her mind was revealed? But 'love' is an imprecise word; it has so many misleading connotations. If I say that my father 'loved' Caroline, or that he was 'in love' with a donkey – the overtones are scandalous and comic, whereas the reality I am trying to describe was neither. It might be more accurate to say that Caroline was as much an object of devotion for my father as she was an object of affection. When he went out to her stable, it was not as a lover hurrying to a tryst, but rather as one of the devout approaching a shrine. He had attained a state of visionary exaltation, of the kind reserved for great lovers and mystics: he had seen the universe in a small grey donkey, and their walks through the streets and alleys of the neighbourhood had the air of a triumphal procession.

My father never spoke directly about any of this, and many of his acquaintances continued to regard the donkey as an eccentric manifestation of the mid-life crises they were suffering. Periodically recalling long-buried fantasies of alternative lives as war correspondents, jazz drummers or professional gamblers, they spent their Saturday afternoons in camera shops and motorcycle dealerships; in the same spirit, they reasoned, my father had acquired a donkey. If he never enlightened them as to Caroline's real significance, it was not through shame or embarrassment, but out of a wish to spare them a painful truth, which they had perhaps already guessed at: he knew he would be forgiven an eccentricity, but not an experience of complete fulfilment that had passed them by.

As for what the donkey felt, I can only speculate. I found it hard enough to read her moods, let alone the secrets of her heart. She combined great personal charm with an air of serene detachment from her surroundings. Her face was wonderfully expressive: the constant motion of her ears, the wrinkling of her muzzle, the flaring of her nostrils, all hinted at a passionate sensibility, but the mild and steady gaze indicated a cooler element in her character. In fact,

I think this ambivalent quality was part of her allure. In company, with a group of my classmates or my father's colleagues clustering round her, she was rather like a great lady of the demi-monde – tantalisingly aloof, graciously accepting the attentions that were paid to her, forever holding out the possibility of greater intimacy, but contriving to keep her admirers at a distance. She certainly showed more interest in my father than she ever did in me or my mother – I think of her coquettish behaviour when we first met her, and her distress at being separated from him. But in the circumstances, to ask whether Caroline reciprocated my father's feelings would be as misguided as to ask whether a princess returns the devotion of her courtiers.

9

This idyllic period of country walks and domestic harmony was surely a just reward for my father's efforts. After all, he had rescued Caroline and brought her back to the city, risking the hardships of the open road and the neighbours' disapproval; he had welcomed her into the family, built her a home with his own hands, and found her gainful employment. But it was precisely at this stage when every obstacle appeared to have been overcome that the whole affair began, slowly but inexorably, to unravel.

During one of their late-night chess games, my father had looked up from the board to see Caroline chewing on one of his captured pawns, and concluded that she was bored. In vain I suggested that she had simply been chewing the pawn as an aid to concentration, the way some people chew the end of a pencil: like all anxious lovers, he was ready to believe the worst. He began to fret about the inadequacy of his game, studying books of openings and tactics in the hope of providing her with more challenging opposition.

But the chewed pawn was just the beginning. Soon afterwards came an incident in the kitchen, when the donkey upset a bowl of egg whites – whether accidentally or on purpose it was not clear, since my mother had her back turned at the time. To my mother this demonstrated only that a professional kitchen was perhaps no place for a donkey. But my father took it as a confirmation of his fears: Caroline had deliberately upset the egg whites in protest against the intellectual poverty of her circumstances – they were stifling her.

'She needs to be stretched,' he said. 'I should have seen it myself. I've read all the literature, there's no excuse. Donkeys' minds are like sponges. They're wonderfully absorbent, very receptive to information, but you have to nourish them – well, what happens to a sponge,' he asked me, 'when you leave it on the edge of the bath?'

'It dries out?' I ventured, slightly bewildered.

'Exactly. It dries out, it shrinks, it gets brittle. This is no life for a creature like her . . . playing amateur chess,' he said indignantly, 'slaving in the kitchen like a drudge.'

'Maybe she misses the office,' my mother said. 'They liked her there – why don't you see if they'll let her have her old job back?'

'I'm not sending her back there to shove bits of paper

around,' my father said, 'poor Caroline, with a dry sponge rattling about inside her head. What she needs is an education.'

And it was in pursuit of this education that my father began, on the days when my mother was working, to take the donkey on excursions all over the city. They toured the local parks, so that she could challenge all comers at chess; they went to the zoo; they attended public lectures; they trudged out to the suburbs to examine sites of historic and archaeological interest; they took the new high-speed rail link to the airport to watch the planes taking off and landing. His avowed aim of improving Caroline's mind – that mysterious organ – might have been taken as an excuse for spending more time alone with her, but there was an air of anxiety and even desperation about him that indicated this was not the case: here was a man increasingly motivated not by self-indulgence, or his avowed concern for the donkey's intellectual development, but by fear of losing her.

This intensive programme of educational activities occupied a considerable amount of my father's time, as I discovered when I asked him to take me to a travelling exhibition of stone axes at the City Museum – I was supposed to be researching a project on Early Man.

'I'm afraid I'm busy with Caroline all this week,' my father told me. 'Tomorrow evening there's a documentary on the Industrial Revolution which I'd like her to see. Thursday is art history night, if you remember.' (My father had bought a set of slides entitled *Masterpieces of Italian Painting* and had taken to projecting a selection of these onto the stable wall on Thursday evenings, with the aim of developing the donkey's colour sense.) 'And on Friday it's ballroom dancing.'

'You're teaching her to dance now?'

'No, we just go to the park and watch people practising. They do it in one of the basketball courts. But it's good for her to get an understanding of rhythm and movement.'

'What about the weekend?'

'Well, I'm taking your mother to the cinema on Saturday afternoon, and on Sunday she's working and Caroline and I are going mushroom picking.'

'Can't I come?'

'We're not just wandering about in the woods with a basket, you know. This is a comprehensive introduction to mycology – we're concentrating on a different group of species every fortnight. Last time it was *Lactarius*, this week we'll be looking at *Russula*. A very tricky genus . . . Frankly, I think you might be a little out of your depth.'

I didn't know what to say to this.

'I'm sorry,' he went on, 'but you see how it is. How about next week, though? I'm free on Tuesday. Why don't I meet you after school, and we can go straight from there to the exhibition.'

But on the following Tuesday, when my last class of the afternoon finished and I made my way to the school gate, my father was not there. I swung my satchel off my shoulder, dropped it on the ground by the railings and squatted down on it to wait. Half an hour later, when the initial flood of children pouring out of the gates had slowed to a trickle of weary teachers, there was still no sign of him. I considered the possibilities. There was no point in going to the museum on my own, because I didn't have any money for the ticket. I decided to look for him at home.

When I got back to the house my father was not there. My mother was out as well; I found a note from her on the kitchen table saying that she had gone out to make a delivery. I went outside and knocked on the stable door, then opened it. There was no one inside. And now, with a sense of shock and betrayal, I understood; he had forgotten all about our trip to the museum and gone off somewhere with Caroline.

It was dark by the time they returned. My father did not come into the house straight away, but spent several minutes fussing about in the yard. I could hear the stable door being unlatched, my father whispering to Caroline and her hooves scraping the concrete. Unable to contain myself any longer, I rushed outside and found him brushing the donkey. Faced with my furious inquisition he put the brush down, and said mildly that he was sorry to have forgotten our arrangement, but he knew something had put the idea of taking Caroline to the museum into his head.

'You took her to the museum?'

'Yes.' And Caroline shifted uneasily from hoof to hoof, as if she understood that she was the cause of this altercation.

'But you were supposed to take me,' I cried. 'What is there for a donkey to see at the museum anyway?'

'I wanted to show her the walrus ivory chess sets,' he muttered.

Naturally, it took me a long time to forgive him for this. But I was surprised to see how angry my mother was, in a way that she had not been after any of his previous adventures. I think she had restrained herself before because she was conscious of the absurdity of seeming jealous of a donkey – but the neglect of a child's education was something over which she felt she could justifiably let herself go.

After this my father began to feel guilty, which he had never done before, over his escapades with Caroline. But he showed no sign of giving them up; indeed, a note of urgency, not to say lunacy, became discernible in the programme – once, when the Austrian state opera came to the city as part of a cultural exchange, he tried to book a box for himself and the donkey at a matinee performance of *Così fan tutte*. To his great regret and my mother's visible relief, no tickets had been available. But it was on a similar impulse that he took her, shortly afterwards, to the open-air cinema.

For a few weeks every summer the City Council would organise showings of films in one of the municipal parks, where a steep grassy bank surrounded by trees formed a natural auditorium. The projector was set up at the top of the bank, and the screen at the bottom – a white cotton sheet with a cord at each corner, the top two stretched between the trees on either side, and the lower two attached to pegs in the ground. This arrangement worked well on still evenings but if there was much of a breeze the picture would tremble and break up, like a reflection in the surface of a lake.

The audience was mostly made up of families with small children, and courting couples. They would arrive as dusk was falling, and spread their rugs and mats on the grass while there was still light enough to see by. Once it was completely dark, the screening would begin.

There were any number of reasons for not taking a donkey to an open-air public showing of *Roman Holiday*, but none of them occurred to my father – he simply felt rather pleased with himself at having found a cultural activity that took place out of doors. It was a mild, balmy evening, and they lingered as they walked through the park: the flowers in the herbaceous borders were in full bloom and the air was scented with jasmine. By the time my father and Caroline arrived at the auditorium a large crowd had already gathered, their faces bathed in the reflected light from the screen, and the film was about to start. The two of them made their way as discreetly as possible to the front of the audience, where my father had noticed an empty patch of grass. But the family immediately behind them complained that the donkey's ears were blocking their view, and they were asked to move. They picked their way carefully round the edge of the crowd and up the bank and installed themselves at the back, next to the projector.

For the next hour or so, my father insisted afterwards, Caroline followed the film with every sign of enjoyment. She pricked up her ears attentively when Audrey Hepburn had her hair cut short, and swished her tail with excitement during the scene in which Gregory Peck pretends to have his hand bitten off by the Mouth of Truth. But at some point she must have begun to lose interest, because she fixed her attention on a salesman with a bucket of cellophane-wrapped roses, who was picking his way round the edge of the crowd. He had not been having much luck; many of the couples who might have bought his roses had already crept off into the woods, and when he reached the back of the crowd his bucket was still practically full.

As soon as he was within reach, Caroline craned forward and began to munch contentedly on the roses. In the darkness, the salesman did not notice straight away what was happening; it was only the loud crackling of the cellophane and the angry shushes which this provoked from the people sitting nearby that alerted him, but by then it was too late. Bellowing with fury, he started hitting Caroline with the empty bucket. She backed hastily away, spitting cellophane, and upset the projector. There was a crash, and before anyone could react, the donkey had bolted down the bank in the darkness, overturning bottles and glasses, stumbling on picnic rugs, with the crowd scattering before her in panic. A few terrified children began to wail. Fearing for her safety, mortified at the disturbance she was causing, my father followed in her wake. At the bottom of the bank, she ran straight into the screen — the cords snapped, and the sheet enveloped her; she blundered on into the woods like a distressed poltergeist, braying fitfully.

My father took advantage of the confusion to catch up with her, disentangled her from the sheet and stroked her trembling flanks until she calmed down. From a safe distance among the trees they watched as the police arrived – Caroline by now unruffled, munching a few leaves of wild garlic, my father simultaneously horrified and exhilarated as he surveyed the results of her delinquency; he clung to her neck as if to steady himself. But his contrition for the criminal damage she had caused was quickly subsumed in a feeling of swelling triumph at having provided her with such a stimulating evening out.

As it turned out, there was very little the police could do except to assess the extent of the damage (a few trampled picnic baskets) and take witness statements. Unfortunately the enveloping darkness and the universal sense of panic had made the citizens even less reliable witnesses than they might otherwise have been. The only person who could have provided a useful account was the flower seller, and he had disappeared as soon as the police arrived in case they asked to see his permit. And after dutifully taking down a few breathless and contradictory accounts of stags in rut, an escaped rhinoceros, a pack of rabid dogs, the policemen decided to go back to the station, put their notes on file, and forget about the whole incident.

None of this had any effect on my father's mood as he led the donkey by a circuitous route out of the woods and home through empty side streets, convinced that he and Caroline were now wanted criminals. A new idea was germinating in his mind; they were truly beyond the pale, fugitives from justice, bound together by their shocking crimes – he had made her his accomplice, or perhaps it was the other way round.

He lay awake late into the night, his brain racing as the fantasy took shape, half-expecting the police to knock on the door at any moment. If he had considered the situation more calmly he would have realised that this was unlikely, but his anxiety was at just the right pitch to disorder his thoughts and stimulate his imagination: they must light out for the territory like Huck Finn, or Bonnie and Clyde – the outlaw couple, living on their wits and sustained only by their love for each other; never sleeping twice in the same bed, somehow managing to keep one step ahead of the authorities . . . Following this train of thought he stumbled across an older, half-formed fantasy; to slip away unnoticed, early one morning – the familiar streets lying exposed and empty in the grey dawn – and begin a new and more congenial life with the donkey somewhere else. They would leave unnoticed and empty-handed, quite casually, as if they were simply going to fetch the morning paper.

Next day my father got up early and went quietly downstairs. Still half-asleep, he pulled on an overcoat over his pyjamas, filled one pocket with oats and the other with raisins from a jar in the kitchen cupboard, then went outside to prepare Caroline for their escape. He opened the front gate. There was no one about in the lane. The air was cool and fresh; it had rained in the night. He stepped back into the yard and unlatched the half-door of the stable. And Caroline, as she did every morning, leant out to sniff the air and thrust her muzzle into his hands — her lovely eyes wide open, candid, innocent, her breath still faintly perfumed with wild garlic.

And immediately, when he saw her there, feet firmly planted in the straw, quite contented, wanting nothing except her breakfast, the idea of flight was plainly absurd; unnatural; impossible. Absent-mindedly he dug in his coat pocket and pulled out a handful of raisins for her. Then he went back inside to boil the water for my mother's tea, and to prepare the real breakfast that Caroline was expecting.

10

One morning not long afterwards, I came downstairs to find the kitchen door standing open. There was nothing strange about this; it generally meant that my father was outside, giving Caroline her breakfast. But when I went out to the yard, the stable was empty; the morning sun shone in through the open door on the straw and concrete. At first I assumed they had gone out for a walk – but if they had, it was odd that her rope and bridle were still hanging in their usual place. Then I noticed that the front gate was open too. It squeaked as I stepped outside and shut it behind me.

For this time in the morning it was unusually quiet. The only sound came from the traffic in the street outside, and the lane was deserted, except for a figure silhouetted at the far end. It was my father.

'She's gone,' he said, without turning round, as I came up

to him. The bucket containing the donkey's uneaten break-fast stood beside him on the tarmac.

My first thought was that someone must have broken in and stolen or kidnapped her. Kidnappings were rare in the city, and for a donkey to be abducted would have been extraordinary; nevertheless I conjured up a picture of Caroline confined in a disused warehouse or a dank cellar and guarded by masked and desperate men. With her mental resilience, I felt, she would have been equal to the ordeal and I imagined her calmly watching her captors as they cut up a newspaper to make a ransom note.

But when I suggested to my father that she might have been kidnapped, he dismissed the idea out of hand. 'They would have taken her bridle and everything else,' he said. 'Anyway, Caroline wouldn't let herself be abducted.'

I didn't see how he could be so sure of this, but I said nothing.

He had seemed quite calm up to this point, almost relieved – I suppose he felt that now the worst had happened at last, he no longer had to fear it. But he was very pale, and suddenly a violent trembling seized him. Perhaps in an attempt to disguise this, he bent down, fished a carrot out of the bucket and began to chew it.

I wanted to help him, to say something reassuring, but I didn't know what to do. 'She can't have gone far,' I said at last. 'We should look for her – maybe someone saw her go.'

'No,' my father said, 'the stable was clean. If she'd been in there all night there would have been dung on the floor. So she must have left just after I shut her in. We'd been going over a few lines in the Sicilian Defence . . .' He took a deep breath and bit off another piece of carrot. 'She could be miles away by now. Besides,' he gestured at the street with what was left of his carrot, 'do you really think we'd find her in all this?' He was right: the morning rush hour was at its height and the traffic was surging past like a river in spate.

We picked up the bucket between us and walked back down the lane in silence. Outside the stable my father paused to point out to me the clean floor, the bridle and nosebag on their hooks, and the chess set on its shelf next to the clock. And prompted perhaps by the sight of these familiar objects, and the thought of all the happy hours he and Caroline had spent there, he set the bucket down; his face contorted strangely, and I went hastily inside to finish my breakfast.

When I came home that evening, my father was nowhere to be found. He had been out all day, my mother said. Only partly reassured by her lack of obvious concern, I went upstairs and tried to start on my homework – we had a maths test at the end of the week. But I found it impossible to concentrate, and after a while I got up and went over to the window. Caroline normally had her dinner at about this time, and the homely noises of the donkey tearing hay from the rack and snuffling and stamping her feet would accompany my mental exertions. I looked down on the forlorn yard and the open door of the empty stable, and decided to abandon my homework for the evening.

I spent the next half-hour making a poster. It was easy enough to find a picture of Caroline and put our address and telephone number underneath, but I hesitated over what to write at the top. 'KIDNAPPED' would not do. 'LOST' implied that we were responsible for her disappearance, while 'WANTED' gave the equally misleading impression that she was a fugitive. At last I settled on 'MISSING'. In the newsagent's at the end of the lane I had some smudgy copies made, and then wandered round the neighbourhood taping the posters to bus shelters and lamp posts. I was sticking the last one onto a telegraph pole outside the newsagent's when I saw my father approaching.

He had spent the day retracing the routes of their favourite walks, questioning shopkeepers and traffic wardens, looking for signs – chewed foliage, heaps of dung – which might indicate that she had passed that way. After this, he rang the city farms, the Animal Refuge and finally – a measure of his confusion and desperation – the university hospital. His mood throughout the day had alternated between fits of trembling and weeping, and a terrible glittery-eyed calm; but just now, he was temporarily overcome with rage – he was returning from the police station, where the officer on duty had refused to add Caroline to the missing persons' register.

He peered at my poster, and became calmer. 'Good work,' he said, 'good work. But I'm afraid it won't be any use.'

'What do you mean?' I said indignantly. 'I spent ages making these.'

'I can see that,' he said, 'and I'm grateful, but how do you think Caroline got out?'

'You mean, if she wasn't kidnapped?'

'She wasn't kidnapped.'

'Well, I suppose you didn't shut her in properly.'

'No,' he said, 'I always shut her in properly.' As we talked, we had been making our way home; now we had nearly reached our front gate, and for the second time that day he took me to inspect the stable. 'She opened the door herself – look, I'll show you.'

The top half of the stable door closed with a latch, which Caroline could easily have lifted with her muzzle and nudged open. There had been another latch on the lower half, but this was broken and the door was fastened with a loop of rope that went through the latch hole and hooked over a bent nail in the door frame. It would have been easy enough for Caroline to bite on the rope and unhook it; he invited me to examine it, a little frayed where she had gripped it in her teeth.

'Well, I don't know why you're looking so surprised,' he said, 'if she can manage six variations on the Bishop's Opening, do you really think she'd have any trouble getting a stable door open?'

But I wasn't surprised; I was taking in the full significance of this new information. When he shut the donkey in each night, he was not really shutting her in; she had stayed only as long as she consented to, and she could have got out whenever she chose. Caroline had not been stolen, or kidnapped, and she had not gone missing either; she had left us.

I caught something of my father's mood. There would be no more evenings doing my homework with the window open, half-listening as Caroline in the yard below tore at a bundle of hay, or snorted as my father talked to her in an undertone, while I struggled with the intricacies of trigonometry or German grammar. No longer would I see her smoky breath over the stable door on cold mornings as I left for school, or hear the clatter of hooves echoing in the alley. The smells of hay and ammonia would fade from the yard, until it was no different from all the others in the street. A string of empty after-school evenings stretched interminably into the future.

In the days that followed, my father continued to scour the city for the donkey. I wasn't sure, after our conversation on that first night, whether he seriously hoped to find her on one of these expeditions – standing in a water meadow, perhaps, or cropping the grass on a railway embankment. Immediately after she disappeared, of course, it felt quite reasonable that he should look for her like this. But as the weeks passed, it became harder to see what justification there was for him to go on searching as he did, decamping to far-flung suburbs in pursuit of increasingly bizarre and dubious leads: the old woman on the allotment who swore that her decimated cabbages bore the imprints of a donkey's teeth, and demanded compensation when he went to investigate; the night he took me to the circus, after reading in the *Evening News* about the donkey that played the cymbals in its Animal Band (it turned out to be a misprinted monkey).

Later he took to browsing at market stalls and second-hand bookshops, the more obscure and out of the way the better, returning with odd volumes – the proceedings of a conference on viral diseases in equines, *A Golden Treasury of Persian Lyrics*, *Chess Openings for the Under-Fives*. It was clear to me by then – although he would never have admitted this – that these expeditions were no longer practical searches for Caroline; they were partly a way of filling the empty days without her, and partly excursions into memory, as he continued to retrace their walks and visit their old picnic sites.

In the same way, his insistence on keeping the stable exactly as Caroline had left it – tack and bridle on their hooks, hay in the rack, water changed and the floor swept daily – had been entirely sensible for as long as it seemed she might reappear at any moment. But as time went on, the place came increasingly to resemble a shrine. Did he still hope that she would return – did he picture himself being roused by the sound of hooves outside, hurrying to the gate, seeing the familiar figure trotting up the lane, running to meet her, falling on her neck? He would sit in the stable for hours, her blanket across his knees, the chessboard set up in front of him, playing through favourite openings of hers or famous matches they had studied together. To the neighbours his incontinent grief over the donkey's disappearance was as bewildering as her first appearance among them had been. Their sympathy was mixed with embarrassment and confusion: it was not a child he had lost, after all. Of course it was sad to lose a pet, but a donkey was hardly a pet – donkeys were livestock, surely? Many of them, too, were secretly relieved. They tried to keep this to themselves, but still I overheard remarks to the effect that she had smelt rather, she did make a lot of noise, and was it really safe to keep a donkey in a built-up area?

As for my mother, she knew better than the neighbours what Caroline had meant to him – all the more so now, as he sat at mealtimes hunched over his plate telling us how much he missed her, or saying that he felt as though he had lost a limb, that she had been his best friend, that there was no one who understood him like she did. Even allowing for the fact that his mind was disordered by grief, this sort of thing could not have been easy for my mother to listen to. All the same, for a long time she was remarkably understanding: she did not even complain when the donkey's blanket appeared on their bed, like a scratchy, musky counterpane. But she must have wondered how long this period of mourning was going to continue; and one day, when she had borrowed some trestle tables for two catering jobs a week apart and my father refused to let her store them temporarily in the stable, her patience finally ran out.

'Where else am I supposed to put them?' she asked.

'Can't you just leave them in the yard?'

'What if it rains?' she said. 'I don't want to leave them outside.'

'All right, what about the kitchen, then?'

'There's no room in the kitchen.'

My father did not look convinced.

'It's only for a few days,' my mother told him. 'I need them again on Tuesday, and they'll be gone after that.'

'It's the thin end of the wedge,' he said. 'It begins with trestle tables, and before you know it the whole stable's crammed with junk. And then where are we supposed to put Caroline?'

'If Caroline comes back, we'll take everything out again,' said my mother, reasonably enough. 'All right then, I'll leave them outside. I just hope it doesn't rain.'

'I'll find a tarpaulin or something to put over them,' he said, but this concession did not draw a response from my mother. 'You're not angry, are you?'

'No,' she said, 'I'm just wondering how you'd react if I was the one who'd disappeared in the middle of the night.'

It was either on the Saturday or the Sunday following this altercation that I accompanied my father on one of his long rambles through the city. It was one of those dismal winter afternoons when the colour seems to have drained out of everything; the sky was lowering, and promised rain, or possibly sleet. But my father had never invited me to go with him before, my mother wanted to spend a quiet afternoon doing her accounts, and I was curious to see exactly where he went on these expeditions and what he did.

At the end of our lane we turned left and walked along the main road for a while, then made our way through a succession of side streets and came out on another wide road. We turned right at the next junction, where I thought I recognised a restaurant on the corner, a grubby white building with plastic palm trees in tubs outside the door. After that I lost all sense of direction, but my father walked with a purposeful air, as if he knew where he was going.

The houses and shops in this part of the city were small and run-down, there were fewer people about, and on the road down which we were walking there were several empty lots, enclosed by high walls plastered with faded posters announcing new retail developments and apartment blocks. From time to time we heard the muffled blast of a ship's siren, to tell us that the river was not far away.

At length we turned off this road and into another street with a small park on one side, where a few trees dripped behind the railings, and on the other side a narrow terrace of shops. I noticed a bookshop, its windows piled high with dusty paperbacks and bundles of magazines; next to it there was a dingy restaurant displaying a plate of fried eggs in the window, and beyond that a launderette, with gouts of steam billowing from the grating by the door and merging with the fog that had started to roll in off the river.

'We'll just have a look in here,' my father said, leading me across the road and into the bookshop. I couldn't tell, from his manner, whether this was the destination he had been making for all along, or whether we had come on it by chance.

The bell jangled as we went in. We were the only customers, but the shop was so small there would not have been room for many more. My father exchanged a few words with the shopkeeper and poked about for a while among the books and papers, briefly examining some back numbers of the *Mule-Driver's Gazette*, before deciding that there was nothing he wanted to buy. We went out; the bell jangled again, and the shopkeeper locked the door silently behind us.

'Are you tired?' my father asked me. 'Let's have a rest before we go back.'

He did not have the air of a man who has made a wasted journey. I followed him obediently back over the road and into the park, where we sat down on the nearest bench.

Except for a man sweeping the steps of the pavilion, the park was empty. The fog was growing thicker by the minute; the trees were fading into silhouettes. And then I noticed: in front of the pavilion the black and white squares of a giant chess board had been painted on the concrete.

'Where are the pieces?' I said.

'No one wants to play in this weather,' my father replied. 'I expect they've all been locked away somewhere.'

A thought struck me. 'Did you ever come here before,' I asked him, 'you know, with Caroline?'

'We went to so many places,' my father said evasively. 'We must have been to all the parks in the city at one time or another.' He contemplated the chessboard for a second and sighed heavily. I waited for him to continue.

'It's funny how some openings have an association with a particular place,' he said at last. 'The Latvian Gambit, for example.'

'I suppose it was invented in Latvia,' I said.

'That's not what I meant,' he said. 'Whenever I come across that opening, it's always this park that I think of. We did come here once, Caroline and me – it was a very hot day, and we played on the board there. It was funny, because she couldn't work out how to move the big pieces at first. She tried picking one up in the usual way, in her teeth, but it was made of foam rubber, and I don't think she can have liked the taste, because she dropped it again. After that she found a way of nudging them into position with her nose and her front hooves.

'Anyway, we played a couple of games, and she beat me easily enough. There was an old man sitting on the bench here watching us, and when we'd finished he asked if he could have a game. He had a walking stick, I remember, and one of his thumbs was bent out of shape by arthritis, and he sat with his hands resting on his stick, and his chin resting on his hands, and when it was his turn he'd call out to me where he wanted to move and I'd pick up the piece and move it for him.

'And Caroline played the Latvian Gambit, and I thought she was making a mistake – it's quite risky, as you know, quite unpredictable. I had my back to her opponent, and I kept signalling to her frantically to try another line. I was getting more and more worried, because I could see how well the old man was playing – you see it more clearly, somehow, when you're moving the pieces yourself. But she ignored me, of course, and she was right. I should have trusted her more. She won the game in the end. That put her in a good mood, and I remember I bought us both an ice cream on the way out – there's a van that parks by the gate in summer.'

He was silent for a moment.

'I should have trusted her more,' he said again. 'Whatever she's doing now, I should trust her to know her own mind.'

'Do you really think you're going to find her now?' I asked, with a directness that startles me now when I remember it.

He considered this for some time. 'I don't know,' he said.

I don't believe I ever saw my father look as downcast as he did then, before or since, and I had the feeling that if I had not roused him he would have gone on sitting there until it got dark.

We started walking back, a different route from the way we had come, first through lanes and alleys, then across a patch of waste ground and out onto a wider road lined with trees. There was hardly anyone about; from time to time a cyclist would materialise, swish past us and dissolve again. The trees in front and behind receded into the fog, each pair smaller and fainter than the last, until they vanished altogether. Neither of us spoke; there was just the raw, slightly chemical damp in the nostrils, and the growing tiredness in my legs.

It felt as though we had been walking for hours when a fruit shop came into view on the street corner ahead of us. Open-fronted, and illuminated with bare bulbs, the place looked from a distance like a lit cavern in the gloomy afternoon.

'Let's get some tangerines for your mother,' my father said, and a man got up from behind a stack of empty crates and started to weigh them out. The electric light blazed off the trays of oranges and pineapples, and glowed through the striped nylon sheeting that had been draped round the entrance to keep the rain from blowing in; bunches of bananas hung from the hooks under the eaves.

My father paid for the fruit, and we carried on walking. It was starting to get dark now. We turned left at the next junction, and to my surprise I saw that we were at the top of our road. A few of the shops were still open, and two waiters were washing dishes outside the restaurant on the corner. We walked up our lane, and as we came in at the gate I saw that the light was on in the kitchen.

'Why don't you take these inside?' my father said, handing me the paper bag of tangerines. 'I'll be with you in a minute.'

I went into the house and found my mother sitting at the kitchen table, doing her accounts.

'Did you have a good walk?' she asked. 'Where did you go?'

'We went to a park,' I told her.

'To a park?' she said. 'In this weather?'

'It was a little cold,' I admitted. 'But we bought some tangerines as well.' I gave her the bag of fruit, and as I did so a noise of bumping and scraping came from the yard.

'What's he doing out there?' she asked.

We went to the window and pulled back the curtain to see my father dragging the trestle tables across the yard and into the stable.

FORM C/32: NOTIFICATION OF MISSING PERSON

Missing person's name (include surname, nicknames, aliases):		CAROLINE	
Date of birth:	NOT KNOWN	**Sex:**	FEMALE
Occupation:		RETIRED	
Eyes:		DARK BROWN	
Hair:		GREY	
Height:		10 HANDS	
Fingerprints available?		Yes (No) Where?	
Any medical conditions:		HOOFS IN NEED OF TRIMMING	
Your contact details:		███████████████	
Nature of relationship to missing person:		PLATONIC	

I imagine Shaw's father handing this document in at the police station, the officer reading through the responses with incredulity, looking at him with some suspicion, and grimly handing him 'Form D27: Lost Property' instead.

On the second page of the form, under the heading 'Distinguishing features', there was more writing:

> 'Her mouth is a casket full of pearls,
> her musky tresses need no scent . . .'

And:

> 'Her eyes are like grapes,
> like narcissi in a garden,
> like the fishpools in Heshbon,
> like two black arrows aimed at my heart.'

I did not think these notes could really have been meant as part of a practical description to help the police in their search. As I read on, I became convinced that they had been written by Shaw's father in a private reverie, after returning from the police station – the fact that they were written with a different pen supported this – and, it seemed, after extensive study of *A Golden Treasury of Persian Lyrics*. And indeed, when I read through that book (which Shaw insisted on lending me), I saw that a number of verses had been underlined:

'And so you have left me and crossed into the Unseen: but which path, which path did you take to leave this world?' (Rumi)

Fascinated and faintly scandalised, I wondered whether Shaw's mother had seen the book, and what she might make of verses like this:

'Tulips and violets and jasmine spring up wherever my beloved plants her feet.'

Or this:

'My companion on every road, the thought of your face.' (Hafiz)

She might, of course, have agreed with the editor of the anthology that they 'express a spiritual yearning in terms of an erotic impulse'. But I couldn't be sure.

Leafing through the 'biographical notes' at the back of the book, I came across the following passage about the life of Rumi, which seemed to me highly significant:

widely regarded as a master of the ghazal, although much of his work also shows the influence of Turkish verse forms.

Rumi was already a highly regarded scholar and poet when, in middle age, he met the wandering dervish Shams of Tabriz. They became inseparable companions, and soon the poet was spending all his nights in 'mystical conversation' with Shams, and neglecting his wife and students. This led to gossip, and growing ill-feeling, and at last one night after dinner Shams went out for a walk and never came back. Rumi spent months searching for his friend, but in vain. Grief-stricken, he retired from public life, occupying himself with his religious devotions and with poetry. He became convinced that the voice of the dervish was speaking through him when he wrote, and it was for this reason that he published all his subsequent poems under the title *The Works of Shams of Tabriz*.

11

Although my father had retired, my mother still had a business to run and in the months after Caroline's disappearance, as the warmer weather arrived, she was busy with wedding receptions and office drinks and garden parties. Often she asked my father to come with her to these functions. It was not just that she needed his help, especially at the bigger events; she did not want to leave him brooding on his own while she was out at work.

My father had never worked in the catering industry before, but he made himself surprisingly useful. Perhaps to compensate for his lack of experience, he was always careful to dress the part, in a neatly ironed white shirt and a black waistcoat and trousers. In addition to helping my mother set up and clear away, he would take people's coats as they arrived, open and pour the wine, and circulate stiffly with trays of drinks and sandwiches. The haggard and grief-stricken look that he had worn in the weeks after Caroline went missing had mellowed into a less alarming expression of private suffering, and this combined with his costume to give him an air of lugubrious formality, reminiscent of a butler or a funeral director, which raised the tone of the proceedings and greatly impressed the guests.

One spring evening I came home from school to find my father, still dressed in his waiter's uniform after one of these events, sitting in a chair outside the front door and reading the newspaper.

'Here,' he said, 'come and look at this.'

There was a kind of choked exultation in his voice; so I was surprised, when I went closer, to see that he was only reading the sports pages. He was pointing at a small photograph, printed between a list of the day's race meetings and a report on a basketball game. It showed, the caption explained, the final of a chess tournament in Smolensk, in western Russia.

It might have been unusual for a newspaper to carry a photograph of a chess game, but I couldn't see that it was a cause for such excitement.

'No,' my father said, 'look in the background, at the spectators.'

I peered at it again. The board and the faces of the players were brightly lit, but the background was in shadow and out of focus, and it was difficult to see much more than a group of figures – some seated, others standing behind them – whom I imagined to be officials and spectators.

'It's Caroline,' he said, 'can't you see? There, on the right.'

In the darkest part of the photograph, next to the group of people, an odd form could just be made out. I would have said at first glance that it was a table on which the players' coats had been piled, but now, looking more carefully, I saw that it was indeed a donkey.

'That's extraordinary,' I said, 'but how do you know it's Caroline?'

'What would a donkey be doing at a chess tournament if it wasn't Caroline?' my father said. 'Be sensible.'

I saw the logic of this, but I found it impossible to tell, from the photograph alone, whether or not the donkey really was Caroline.

My father was convinced. That evening he called the newspaper and ordered a print of the photograph; he also asked if the photographer could provide any information about the donkey in the background. The print arrived a few days later, accompanied by a note from the photographer. He agreed that the figure on the right gave the impression of being a donkey, but he had not noticed it at the time he took the picture – he had naturally been concentrating on the board and the players, which were his main subject. Nor could he remember having seen a donkey in the audience at any other point. However, the event had taken place in a sports hall just outside the city, so it was conceivable that in such a rural setting an animal might have strayed in – there had been people selling eggs and vegetables outside the entrance, and it might have belonged to one of them. He couldn't say how strict the authorities were about the admission of spectators to these tournaments – he did not usually cover sporting events, and had been in the area on another assignment.

This was not exactly a positive confirmation of the donkey's presence in the photograph, but neither was it a denial. Even from the enlarged print, though, I found it impossible to identify the donkey with any certainty. All the same, there was no doubt in my father's mind. 'Look at the way she's standing,' he said. 'Look at her ears. They're both pointing forward, but she's holding the left one slightly higher than the right. She always did that when she was concentrating.' I think also that the poetic rightness of it – that a donkey at a chess tournament could only be Caroline – made practical questions, such as how she had found her way to Russia, unimportant. He had the picture mounted and set in an ornate gilt frame.

Anyone hearing about this episode at second hand would be hard put not to conclude that my father had finally lost his mind. But it never occurred to me at the time that he might be mad. He was so utterly firm in his convictions, so reasonable in his tone, that I was inclined to believe him: in my father's presence the laws of logic were stretched and bent, rather as light bends in the gravitational field of a star. I questioned the evidence, but not his sanity.

'It's quite clear now,' he announced, after he had returned from the framer's with the picture and was showing it proudly to me and my mother. 'Caroline wanted to compete at the highest level. There was nothing more I could do for her – I could provide the loving home environment, but not the mental stimulation. It's that pragmatic intelligence and the ability to look out for herself. Typical of her, typical of a donkey. She'll be a grandmaster before long, I'm sure of it.'

'But she wasn't actually playing in that tournament,' I pointed out.

'No, of course,' my father said, 'she was studying form. You can learn a certain amount from the record of a game, but the only way really to see what goes through the players' minds is to watch the matches as they happen.'

After this he would hurry to get hold of the paper every morning, and turn first to the sports pages – checking, I supposed, for reports of Caroline's entrance onto the professional circuit. I had been unable to decide how much of the donkey's contribution to my father's firm had been real and how much of it a species of group hallucination, but I was sure that her new career as a would-be chess grandmaster was a complete delusion, of the kind entertained by people everywhere who console themselves over an unbearable loss with the thought that their loved one has gone to a better place. My father's vision of Caroline's new life may have been more idiosyncratic, but it was essentially the same delusion.

And so I was not surprised to see him, in the weeks that followed, scanning the sports pages with an air of private delight, as if he were reading a love letter, and not an account of match-fixing in badminton or the national water polo team's latest humiliation. But one evening I found him sitting at the kitchen table in front of the chessboard, with a sheet of newspaper spread out beside it, one hand resting on a knight, the index finger of the other marking a place on the paper.

I went and looked over his shoulder. The newspaper wasn't a local one – in fact, it was printed in the Cyrillic alphabet.

'Is it Russian?' I asked.

'It is.'

'But you can't speak Russian.'

'That doesn't matter,' my father said. 'I'm looking at this.' He tapped the paper.

Near the foot of the page, printed very small and hemmed in by advertisements, was a chess problem. 'So they have those in Russian newspapers too,' I said. 'Where did you get this, anyway?'

I didn't think it could have come from the newsagent's at the end of the lane – the *Evening News* and a few women's magazines were about as far as it went.

'It came in the post,' he said, 'but never mind about that now. Just look at this position – White to move and win.'

I studied the chess notation dutifully, but the numbers and letters were as impenetrable to me as the Russian. 'It looks difficult,' I said, 'but you know I don't really understand these things . . .'

'It's Caroline's,' my father cried, 'd7! and White mates in two. Mate by promotion – it's one of her specialities. Don't you remember?'

'Are you sure?'

'Of course,' he said. 'Maybe you don't see it – you're not a chess player, after all – but it's exactly her style: the grace of a dancer, the force of a juggernaut. I'd know it any-where – it's as clear as a signature, the angel.'

I grappled with the implications of what he was telling me, trying to picture Caroline as a roving chess correspondent.

'Do you think she's working for this paper, then?' I asked.

'The *Novgorodskaya Gazeta*,' he said absently. 'I doubt it – a provincial newspaper wouldn't be enlightened enough to employ a donkey. Most likely it's one of those set-ups where they get the readers to send in the problems.'

'But even if Caroline set the problem,' I said, 'who sent you the paper?'

'Caroline did,' my father said. 'At least, I don't really see who else it could have been.' He handed me the envelope that the sheet of newspaper had come in. It was empty.

'Wasn't there a letter with it?'

'No, just the paper.'

I examined the envelope. It had a Russian stamp, and our address was printed on it in pencil. 'Is that her hand-writing?'

'Perhaps it is a bit far-fetched,' he admitted, 'but when I look at this problem – it's Caroline's style, there's no doubt about that.'

Leaving aside the question of whether Caroline really was contributing chess problems to a provincial Russian news-paper, I wondered for some time after this who had sent the cutting. I couldn't believe it had been Caroline, whose duties in the office, so far as I knew, had never included stamping or addressing letters. On the other hand, as my father said, it was hard to see who else it could have been. For a while I was sure that it must have been our neighbours, who had recently been on a package tour to Moscow and St Petersburg, but the postmark was not from either of these cities, and as they didn't speak Russian themselves I didn't see why they would have bought the newspaper in the first place.

'So what will you do?' I asked, 'go to Russia and look for her?'

My father glanced up from the newspaper. 'I know better than that,' he said. 'If she doesn't want to be found, do you think I'd ever find her? No, I'm going to subscribe to this newspaper.'

So the chessboard took up permanent residence at one end of the kitchen table, a constant reminder of the donkey's existence, and every fortnight a packet would arrive containing twelve copies (there was no Sunday edition) of the *Novgorodskaya Gazeta*. He rationed himself to one copy a day, and every morning after breakfast he would settle down in front of the chessboard and apply himself to that day's problem.

A glance at the paper was usually enough to tell him whether it had been set by Caroline or by 'some halfwit with a head full of sand', as he put it. Some days he only needed ten or fifteen minutes to solve it; on other days he would turn the problem over in his mind for hours, dashing back to the paper in the evening to scribble down the solution with a flourish.

All this time my father was engaged on the sprawling,

interminable piece of writing which he referred to variously as a memoir, a study, a report, and a history, but which is not really adequately described by any of those titles. He had moved a desk and an old office typewriter into the stable, where he also accumulated a great pile of books and papers, picked up at the city's second-hand bookshops and flea markets. He used to spend hours out there, and I would hear him pounding away at the typewriter keys at odd times of the day and night, but I often wondered how much progress he was actually making.

It was not just the uncertainty over the title, which indicated to me a certain lack of focus; his working methods were haphazard, to say the least. He used to scribble his notes on the back of old policy documents, on envelopes, in the margins of the newspaper, and the whole project seemed to disintegrate nearly as fast as he put it together. From time to time stray pages would turn up in the biscuit tin, or stuffed behind the pipes in the airing cupboard, and for several years his unfinished monograph on the effects of ragwort poisoning propped up the short leg of the kitchen table.

He was not secretive about his research interests; he was happy to discuss humane methods for harnessing draught animals, or biblical references to the donkey, or the superiority of its hearing to that of the horse, with anyone who cared to listen. But if you asked him about the progress of his work, or when he expected to finish, he became cagey and defensive. At the time I took this as an admission that he was getting nowhere, but reflecting on it now I think he reacted in this way because he saw the question as misguided. There was no progress to be made. This thing to which he was devoting his energies was not a project, with a timetable and a completion date. It was a purpose, a cause; something to live for.

To her credit I think my mother understood this before I did, and although she liked to refer to the work somewhat dismissively as his 'magnum opus' – which incidentally may have been a more suitable title than any he came up with – she did not grudge the time he spent on it. Indeed, on one occasion she even accompanied him to a conference on equine preventative medicine at the Veterinary College, where he intended to give a fringe presentation on the subject of saddle sores. When they arrived at the venue, however, my father discovered that he had brought the wrong piece of paper with him. According to my mother, he was not visibly perturbed by this, and he read quite happily and animatedly from the paper he had brought on 'Images of the Donkey in Etruscan Art' until the room had emptied and only she was left applauding in the front row.

After the funeral, when we were sitting at the kitchen table and sorting through his more mundane papers, such as bank statements and pension slips, my mother reminded me of this story. It was then that I asked her if anything was left of the great work. She sat back in her chair and considered briefly, then told me to look in the bottom drawer of the dresser.

I did as she said; the drawer was heavy, and awkward to

open. When I finally pulled it out I found it contained a pile of carefully folded tablecloths and tea towels, and underneath them the bundle of papers that you've already seen, tied up with green legal tape.

I was astonished. I always assumed that my father's work had been lost, like so many other things from my childhood, or else that it couldn't amount to more than a few scraps of paper. But there must have been several hundred pages here. 'He kept everything, then?' I said, as I untied the tape and started leafing through the papers at the top of the pile, the sheets of typescript, the photocopies and handwritten notes and newspaper clippings.

'He didn't keep it,' my mother said. 'I did.'

In the last few years of my father's life, being out of the country so much, I didn't get home very often. But when I did, nothing had changed. He still took my mother's breakfast up to her in the mornings – less steady on the stairs as the years passed, shuffling in his slippers, the teacup and spoon rattling on the tray. It was a modest existence, but there was nothing broken or pathetic about him. I would find him, mid-morning, still in his pyjamas, lying on the sofa cushions which he had arranged on the floor, watching gymnastics on television, but with great concentration and relish, as if this were a princely entertainment – as if there were nothing in the world that he would rather have been doing.

Caroline was never far from his thoughts – often, when we were talking in the yard together about his and my mother's holiday plans, or working overseas, or a paper he had just read on the economic impact of the donkey on agriculture in tropical regions, his attention would wander in the direction of the empty stable, and I would know he was thinking of her. But I never caught in his expression, or in an unguarded remark, the gnawing sense that life had passed him by; something that could not be said for many of his contemporaries, or for many of mine. And when visitors came to the house, they were met not with the wild stare of a lunatic, or the wandering gaze of someone lapsing into senility, but with a look of piercing and disconcerting sanity.

Even his dress, which to the insensitive observer might have suggested an old man letting himself go (sweater gone at the elbows, bedsocks stuffed into galoshes, haphazardly shaven chin), seemed to me like nothing so much as a demonstration of the sage's magnificent disregard for external appearances. And the last time I came home – the last time I saw him – he opened the door to me, gathering the flaps of his dressing gown round him like robes of state, with an air that I can only describe as triumphant.

It is a strange feeling, having set myself the task of putting together a few notes on Caroline's remarkable career, to be typing these words in the very place where so many of her best games were played, the old shed which for me at least has become one of the sacred places of chess, like the Café de la Régence where Voltaire and Napoleon played, or Simpsons in the Strand, the scene of the 'Immortal Game' between Anderssen and Kieseritzky, or the old Manhattan Chess Club.

I think it is fair to say that no one who saw Caroline play will ever forget the experience. She had an uncanny grasp of positions, and the ability to produce combinations apparently out of nothing. But despite her undoubted technical strengths, her style was beautifully simple. Its chief characteristic was its lucidity - it was clear as rainwater. And it was innate, organic; a style that grew naturally as leaves on a branch.

Watching her take on unwary strangers, I would be reminded of the story about a certain distinguished general, hero of the Mexican War, author of a manual on infantry tactics, and chess amateur, who visited Morphy's home town of New Orleans and asked for a game with a strong local player. When the nine-year-old Morphy was fetched, the general stormed out in a rage, thinking he was being made fun of. But eventually he was mollified and persuaded to return to the board where the little boy was waiting patiently. Morphy proceeded to demolish the general, twice, without turning a hair; the second time forcing mate after six moves. Caroline was cut from the same cloth.

She had no use for the methodical study of openings so popular with club players these days and her opening play was often quite casual, not to say reckless. In one memorable game she astounded and unsettled her opponent by using her first eight moves to push each of her pawns forward by one square. But from this apparently insane beginning there emerged a combination of extraordinary power which brought her a decisive victory. If she was not a natural student of openings, all the same she was a capable exponent of the Ruy Lopez and she demonstrated several important flaws in the French Defence, while there was a particular variation in the Catalan Opening that she played so often I thought of naming it after her, until I learnt that it had already been named after Alekhine.

There are countless anecdotes about the behaviour of the great players at the board. Steinitz would walk away five or six paces and stride up and down, his head bowed in thought. Tartakower liked to sit bolt upright, dragging his fingers through his long beard and staring at the pieces, while Capablanca would go to the other end of the room and chat easily with an acquaintance while he waited for his opponent to move. As for Caroline, she used to stand quite still, her head lowered almost bashfully. If the position was a complex one, she might turn aside and tug a mouthful of hay from the rack on the wall. By the time she had finished munching, she would be ready to make her move.

In the open air she often felt the pressure more, but she did her best not to show it. Playing in the local park she always liked to walk round and round a certain bush or dip her head in the fountain between moves. I remember one particular game in which, faced with a strong Slav Defence, she backed away from the board and spent a few minutes rubbing herself against a corner of the bandstand, returning to play an admirable 6. Ne5. Really, to watch her playing was an aesthetic experience, and when I faced her myself I was always torn between watching her and concentrating on my next move.

But it seems to me that what distinguishes the great players from the rest is above all a quality of vision. I mean the ability to see deeper as it were into reality than other people - to look at an unpromising position and perceive at once the beautiful combination, miraculous and yet apparently inevitable, or the devastating single move that changes the whole course of play. In the same way, a novice might pore for hours over the annotated moves of an Evergreen or an Immortal Game without grasping the marvels, the wit, the profundity, contained in those columns of numbers and letters.

I liked to quote Morphy to her — that prodigy who gave up chess for a dismal career in the law. 'To me,' Morphy once said, 'the opening matters only because it leads to the endgame, as the dressing room matters only because it leads to the stage.' Or else I would ask, 'What use is a happy beginning without a happy ending?' a remark attributed to Emanuel Lasker. And metaphorically, I think, if not literally, we understood each other very well. She demonstrated a profound knowledge of endings, and like Capablanca she was a virtuoso of the endgame. (This is partly why I find it so hard to believe she did not know exactly what she was doing that night when — But I have been over this a thousand times.)

As Marshall said of Capablanca, 'His games will be his everlasting memorial.' But I do not want to sound too final a note. I am not writing an obituary, but an appraisal of Caroline's career to date, and it may be that her greatest achievements are yet to come.

12

The restaurant was almost empty now; the lunch hour had ended some time ago. I poured out a cup of lukewarm tea and drank it, conscious all the while of Shaw watching me nervously.

'I suppose you can imagine why I've told you all this,' he said.

As a matter of fact, I had no idea, but he lost no time in explaining.

'Well, I'd like to know what really happened to Caroline – I've often wondered about it.'

'I thought you said she went to Russia.'

'It's possible. But I'd like to be certain. Anyway, I thought you might be able to help me.'

'I'm a journalist,' I told him, 'not a private detective.'

'I know,' he said, 'but you could look through your paper's archives and see if there was anything that might be relevant. Any stories – any clues . . .'

It was an odd thing to ask. I looked at him carefully: I

wondered if he might have inherited something of his father's obsession. I didn't think it likely that anything about a missing donkey would have made it into the paper. All the same, I promised to see what I could find out.

The waiter had been eyeing us for a while; now he came over to our table with the bill, and Shaw was suddenly apologetic: he had made me late, I must want to get back to my office, he was sure I was busy. I told him it didn't matter, but he insisted on paying for our lunch.

We went out together into the dank afternoon, through the streets of low houses, with their absurdly narrow pavements, the rows of harshly pollarded plane trees still retaining most of their leaves, even this late in the year – they had gone grey, not brown, as if they had petrified instead of dying in the usual way. We kept up a desultory conversation as we walked back to the subway – to tell the truth, I didn't pay much attention to what he was saying. I was wondering about his motives for getting in touch with me. Had he really gone to all this trouble – the story, the lunch – just to ask me this relatively simple favour? And surely he could have arranged to go through the paper's archives himself? He did not have the air of a man weighed down by an unanswered question; on the contrary, he seemed light-hearted now, relieved even, as if he had just got something off his chest. And it occurred to me that perhaps it was the other way around – the favour had been an excuse to tell the story.

When we reached the subway entrance Shaw stopped, and stuck his hand inside his jacket. 'I almost forgot,' he said, fishing an envelope out of his pocket. 'I wanted to show you this.'

I backed out of the way of the people streaming down the

steps and had a cursory look inside the envelope. It was full of photographs.

'My father took them,' he said. 'I found them at the bottom of the wardrobe when we were going through his things.'

There were a few pictures of Shaw and his mother; one of them standing together in what I assumed was their front yard, one of his mother sitting on a picnic rug, smiling and shielding her eyes from the sun, and a school photograph of Shaw wearing a white shirt and tie. There were also several shots of a donkey that I took to be portraits of Caroline. They did not have the air of posed photographs. They looked as though they had been snapped in haste, with little regard for composition or background. In many of them her head, or a leg, was blurred where she had moved as the picture was being taken.

As for the rest, they were mostly views of the city; a few that I recognised, including one of the office building that had until recently been visible from my window, but many more that I did not. There was little of obvious interest in them, no sights or landmarks. They were strangely impersonal, like photographs of a crime scene. I guessed that Shaw's father had taken them in the same way – I mean after the event, during his long solitary walks through the city after Caroline went missing.

'Why don't you keep them?' Shaw said, when I went to hand them back. 'They might help with identification – you know, in case you find a picture or something.'

Privately I doubted that they would – to me, one donkey looks much like another, and I couldn't even have said whether it was the same animal in all the photographs. Perhaps he was hoping they would convince me that his story was true. But I just nodded, and put the envelope in my pocket. He thanked me for listening to him; I thanked him for lunch, and he shook my hand, turned and hurried down the steps.

When I got back to the office, I went down to the basement to look through the archives. Shaw had given me the exact date of the donkey's disappearance – which he remembered easily, he said, because his father had always marked the anniversary with a vase of thistles on the kitchen dresser. The following evening's edition had been largely given over to the details of a financial scandal in the town hall, but on the inside pages I found a brief report of a traffic accident: a man leading a donkey across one of the new expressways just outside the city had been run down by an articulated lorry laden with scaffolding poles. It had been early evening, and in the failing light the driver had not seen them. According to the report, they had both been killed instantly. Neither of the victims had been identified – which is to say that the man had not been identified. But the donkey had been carrying sacks of cement, which suggested that they might have been on their way to the fish farm over the road, where one of the tanks was cracked.

It was possible that I was reading a report of Caroline's death. On the other hand, there were surely other donkeys in the city, especially in that marginal area of waste ground and builders' yards and market gardens on its outskirts. More to the point, it was hard to see how Caroline could have found a new owner and been pressed into service several miles away within the space of a few hours, when she had only left the stable the night before. I had to conclude that the article did not prove anything very much. At the same time, the lack of proof did not seem to matter. What Shaw had told me was not a story requiring the meticulous checking of facts; it was more like something out of the sagas, or the lives of the saints. His father undoubtedly belonged in the company of those exemplary and heroic figures. As I looked round at my office with the trailing plants in the corner, the desk shedding papers like a moulting animal and, outside the window, the construction work still proceeding at a furious pace under floodlights, I thought of him with envy and admiration. And it was in that spirit that I decided to record the story. I began by making notes in idle moments at my desk, but as the story took shape I found myself working on it in the evenings when I came home, often well into the night.

When it was finished, I thought of sending a copy to Shaw, but I realised that he had omitted (out of absent-mindedness, I suppose) to leave me his address. I didn't think he would really be disappointed not to hear from me; all the same, I was sorry not to be able to return the manuscript, or the photographs. One afternoon I spread them out on my desk and studied them. It struck me that they would add something to the account I had written, not so much as illustrations – Shaw's father was an indifferent photographer – but to provide a sort of window onto his mind.

I cleared my desk, slipped the strange account into a file along with the manuscript and took it down the corridor to the editor's office. He had gone home hours ago, but the door was open. On an impulse, I went in and left the file on his desk. Then I fetched my coat and went down into the street.

As I made my way home, I was still turning the story over in my mind. In the office I had felt slightly foolish, reckless even, handing it in as if it was just another report on unemployment figures or share issues or municipal elections. But there in the street, it no longer seemed out of place: in this city, private and public life, the ordinary and the fantastic, are mingled everywhere you look. Even on the great shopping streets, where the heavy stone portals of the banks alternate with glass-fronted department stores whose windows and floors are constantly swabbed and polished, the grand commercial facade is pierced at intervals by the dark entrance to a lane, down which you glimpse a line of washing, some gas bottles, a dusty tree . . . There are lanes like this all over the city, but here they contrast so sharply with the surging tides of traffic, the evening crowds overflowing the pavements, the shop lights and the neon glowing in the smoggy dusk, that they seem like entrances to another world, and it would have been no surprise to see a man and a donkey emerge from one of the archways and vanish into the rush-hour traffic, like an apparition from an old story.

Acknowledgements

Thank you to Charles Collier, Stuart Williams, Matthew Dixon, Pam Rhodes, Simon Rhodes, Lizzie Strickland and the London Print Studio.